Leander Talbot's life changed forever when his wife died. He is now reluctantly venturing back into society, knowing that, as the Earl of Ockley, he must marry again to produce an heir. But he can't bring himself to the sticking point. Instead, he spends his time evading the matchmaking mamas of the ton.

The dark and dangerous Duke of Arden is an infamous libertine. It is said that he seduces innocents, and there are even more sinister tales whispered of his predilections. Only the wild young blades who form his retinue know the truth, but he is shunned by all save those wishing to court notoriety.

A chance meeting brings Leander into Arden's orbit. Ignoring the warnings about Arden's intentions, Leander is drawn into a seductive world of sexual indulgence. There, he finds the freedom he craves from his overbearing family. By the time he suspects Arden might have ulterior motives, it may be too late to save his reputation — and his heart.

The Earl's Awakening
Copyright © 2023 Joy Lynn Fielding
ISBN: 978-1-4874-3907-1
Cover art by Martine Jardin

Published by eXtasy Books Inc

Look for us online at:
www.eXtasybooks.com

The Earl's Awakening

By

Joy Lynn Fielding

DEDICATION

CHAPTER ONE

Leander consulted his pocket watch and found to his dismay that it was not yet midnight. Many more hours of purgatory lay before him. He knew his mother would not consent to leave until the ballroom was almost empty, and there appeared no prospect of that happening soon. The centre of the room was filled with couples engaged in a country dance while other guests occupied almost every gilt chair set against the walls.

The ballroom had grown stifling as the night wore on. Floral arrangements wilted in the heat, filling the air with the cloying scent of hyacinths and mimosa. Leander was thankful he had possessed the forethought of tying his cravat in an Osbaldeston as he was not in such straitened circumstances as some gentlemen, who were red-faced and perspiring. He could, however, feel sweat prickling in the small of his back. This determined him that he had done his duty as a guest and might now retreat to the cooler climes of the card room.

Unfortunately, he had made his decision too late, for his hostess was approaching. Lady Kempe was fanning herself vigorously, her gaze fastened to his face in a way that betrayed he was the object of her purposeful stalking. He was thankful for the movement of air from her fan as she reached him, although he wished she were taller so that he might feel the breeze upon his face.

"Lord Ockley," she said. "May I present you to Miss Westcourt?"

Knowing that her query was not so much a question as a

directive, Leander murmured agreement. Lady Kempe manoeuvred him towards a young lady who had violets threaded through her hair, complementing her lilac crepe dress. She was conscious of their approach if Leander was not mistaken, although she only looked up when Lady Kempe spoke.

"The Earl of Ockley, Miss Westcourt." Having made this introduction, Lady Kempe swept away to perform similar duties for another unfortunate couple.

"How do you do, Miss Westcourt?" Leander forced himself to smile at her. It was not Miss Westcourt's fault that he would rather be in Hades than have to stand up for another dance.

And, he owned, if he had to have a partner, at least Miss Westcourt was a pleasant one. Her figure was trim, her hair golden blonde, and her eyes dark blue. More importantly, she maintained a flow of sensible conversation as they came together in the set and, unlike some of the other young ladies with whom he'd danced, she did not hold his hand an instant longer than was seemly. Neither did she betray disappointment when, having returned her to a seat, he left her once more.

He did not linger in the crowded ballroom but took himself to the card room. There, with a sigh of relief, he joined some gentlemen for a hand of whist. He knew that he should not regret the generous impulse that had led him to accompany his mother this evening, for he was aware of her deep concern about his brother Henry, even now fighting against Napoleon. Every week, it seemed, brought news from overseas of acquaintances dead from battles or disease. Each time the dowager countess heard these accounts, her eyes grew darker and her need for diversion more urgent. Leander felt it incumbent upon him to distract her. That did not mean he had to enjoy the experience.

He was immeasurably relieved when, finally venturing

back into the emptying ballroom, he was summoned to his mother's side.

"I have ordered the carriage to be brought, Leander," she said. "I hope I do not disturb your time with Miss Westcourt."

Leander was so pleased to hear of their imminent departure that he could not bring himself to be concerned that it was his carriage and servants with which his mama was making free. Sometimes he wished Bella had not had such a tender heart, for it had been her wish that the dowager continue to live in the house in Green Street during the Season and in the main residence at Ockley rather than removing to the Dower House. He had levelled a quizzical look at his wife when she proposed this arrangement. She'd explained that, with Henry likely to be sent overseas with his regiment, it would be cruel to leave the dowager so isolated. She had added ruefully that she expected the dowager would spend all her time visiting them in any case, so it would make little difference. And now that Bella was gone, along with the child she had longed for, perhaps his mama's company was better than living in that cold townhouse alone.

He handed his mother up into the carriage and tucked a rug around her knees to ward off any chill from the April night air before taking his seat.

"How did you find Sophia?" she asked. "I think her a delightful child, very properly behaved. It is so provoking of her uncle Radcliffe to die when he did, for it caused her to miss the beginning of the Season."

Leander, who'd been thinking of nothing more than looking forward to his bed, frowned. "Who?"

"Sophia Westcourt, Lady Annesley's daughter. She's an heiress, you know."

Leander's jaw tightened as he returned his gaze to the dark streets through the window of the carriage. "She was pleasant company," he said, for anything else would be ungallant.

"She is most well-regarded," his mama said.

Leander knew from experience that she would continue in this vein for the entirety of their journey if he did not put a stop to it. "I am not looking for a new wife, Mama," he said firmly.

She nodded in acknowledgement, but she would not let the subject lie. "I am not insensible of your feelings on the matter, yet you must have an heir."

He breathed deeply to calm his unfurling temper. Not quite two years had passed since Bella's death, but his mama had been attempting to see him wed since the beginning of the Season. "If I die tomorrow, Henry will inherit."

"Should your brother survive the dangers he faces each day." The dowager's voice trembled and she turned her face away. Cursing silently, he laid his hands upon hers, clasped tightly in her lap. Clumsy fool, to remind her of her worst fear.

"You know how Henry is," he encouraged her gently. "There is not a Frenchman alive who has his measure."

She caught his wrist. "Oh, I do hope not." A sob broke from her. "You don't know what it's like, Leander, to spend each day wondering . . ."

"Did he not say in his letter that he was hopeful for a swift return?" he asked, as her voice trailed away. "We may yet see him soon." His mother's grasp lost its desperate edge, and he knew she took comfort from the prospect.

Leander could not truthfully say that he did the same. He found himself staring into the looking glass long after his valet had left him that night. The face that looked back at him was one he scarcely recognised. His hair was brushed à la Brutus, as it had been for the last few years, and its colour still reminded him of his dark chestnut mare. But his high cheek-bones seemed more prominent these days and his lips more generous, as if the strain he'd been under had melted away extraneous flesh. It was his eyes, however, that held his

4

attention. They had always been a nondescript brown, regardless of Bella's fancy that they contained amber flecks, but there was now darkness in them, absorbing any softness that might once have lingered. It struck him that he looked weary, and older than the twenty-five years he had been on this earth.

And all the less able to cope with his younger brother, Henry. Theirs had always been a difficult relationship. Despite the two years that separated them, they had followed tradition and gone up to Eton at the same time. The masters had been swift in their unfavourable comparisons of the two, just as their mother had been. Henry had performed heroic sporting feats, becoming a popular football player and an expert boatman, and had finally captained the first eleven. Unbelievably, some of the older boys had clamoured to join his prized circle of intimates. The naturally introspective earl had been overshadowed in every way. Though he tried desperately not to care, Henry's easy-going contempt of his older sibling's quieter character had flicked him on the raw.

In his more charitable moments, Leander wondered if Henry's insufferableness might be due to concerns of his own. Perhaps he set out to impress everyone with his heroic feats — first sporting, now military — due to the whispers about his parentage. The match between their parents had not been a happy one. Leander's father had been a quiet gentleman, preferring to spend his time at the family's extensive estate. There, he oversaw the management of the estate and spent the rest of his time in his library with his beloved Greek and Latin texts. His new wife, on the other hand, had discovered how it felt to have London at her feet. As an accredited Beauty, allied to one of the oldest families in the land, the *ton* was hers. To spend her time immured in the country had not been much to her liking, and she had let her husband know of her unhappiness in no uncertain terms.

Leander's father had passed away in the present earl's third year. His was a sudden death, precipitated, so the rumours went, by the discovery of the true paternity of the younger boy. Malicious gossip claimed that Henry had been sired by one of the royal dukes, although the countess had continued to be welcomed in society by even the very highest sticklers. Who would risk offending one who apparently held the ear — along with other appendages — of royalty? Leander dismissed such talk as baseless, although he could not help but notice that, of the two sons, only he had been christened according to his father's ruling passion.

When he finally climbed between his sheets, Leander blew out his candle and decided to give his brother no more thought. There was no certainty that Henry would be returning home. If that were to happen, well, it would please their mama. For that at least he could be thankful.

CHAPTER TWO

The following day, Leander visited Tattersall's. He was thinking of buying a new hunter to replace Spartan. The gelding's enthusiasm for the chase remained undimmed, but his age was beginning to concern Leander. Surveying the cattle in the stables, he thought he might use Spartan for the first stage of the hunt and simply change horses sooner than usual. He reflected, not for the first time, that Bella's soft heart had been contagious. Inconveniencing himself over an old horse's enjoyment was not something he would previously have considered.

"Ockley!"

He turned at the call to find Jack Sittingbourne approaching. He looked immaculate as always, in a dark green coat, biscuit-coloured pantaloons, polished Hessians, and a curly brimmed beaver hat.

"I have not seen you this age," Jack declared, as he reached Leander and clasped his shoulder in greeting. "I almost thought you had retired to the country."

"Perhaps, as a newly married man, you are the one who has been infrequently abroad of late," Leander said. Little more than a month had passed since Jack had married Olivia Peabody.

Jack's smile in response looked somewhat automatic and did not touch his eyes. Leander wondered at that. They had been friends since Oxford, and he knew Jack to be an easygoing gentleman who was not often out of humour.

"My presence is rarely required now that Mrs

Sittingbourne is a married lady," Jack said. He then pressed his lips firmly together, as if he'd said too much.

Leander found himself at a loss. Jack had never professed undying love for the Peabody girl — her fortune was a slightly different matter — but they had seemed to enjoy one another's company. Perhaps Leander had been mistaken and their marriage had never been anything more than a trade that ensured money for Jack and status for Peabody. Leander knew that he and Bella had been most unfashionable in finding such enjoyment in one another's company for the all-too-brief year their union had lasted, but the bitten-down disappointment in Jack was hard to miss.

"What do you think of the bay?" Leander asked after a pause. "He looks to be a little narrow-chested, yet there is something about him I like."

The awkward moment passed, and they fell to talking of horseflesh. This conversation occupied them as they inspected every animal in the stables. Their discussion looked set to continue the rest of the day until Jack remembered he had an appointment with Gentleman Jackson. Leander was briefly tempted to accompany him to the boxing saloon but could not quite summon the enthusiasm, so they parted ways.

Leander wandered somewhat aimlessly back to Green Street. He still could not make up his mind about the bay. A raw-boned young grey had also drawn his attention, but the fire in its eyes that had so attracted him had translated to restlessness and belligerence when trotted out by one of the grooms. He felt the beast had great promise if someone were to spend the time bringing it along, but he did not know if he had the patience and interest necessary for the task. It would have to be the bay.

He was still ruminating on the amount he would be willing to bid at Monday's sale as he mounted the steps to his front door.

"My lord, Captain Talbot has arrived, not ten minutes since," his butler informed Leander as he took his hat and gloves. "Captain Burnage accompanies him."

Thanking Pickett for this unwelcome intelligence, Leander schooled his features into a welcoming expression and climbed the stairs to the drawing room. He found the dowager flitting between her younger son and his friend, exclaiming over and over her relief at seeing them unhurt.

Leander stood in the doorway, observing. Henry was in regimentals, which made his already large figure appear to dwarf the well-appointed room. He was taller than Leander, and broader, with dark blond hair, a firm jaw, and clear blue eyes. Thomas Burnage was shorter and more slender, his untidy blond curls reflecting the restlessness of his nature, which meant he was forever seeking new diversions. He was Henry's constant companion. The two had been inseparable since meeting at Eton and three years previously had bought their commissions together.

Leander watched for a moment longer as his mother looked up at Henry, her face animated in a way he had not seen for a long time, her delicate features lit with excitement and pleasure. Henry smiled back at her in full good humour until he became aware of Leander's presence.

"Lea!" They clasped hands warmly, Leander repeating the ritual with Burnage.

Leander wanted to question the two returned soldiers on developments in the war but could not find an opening amidst his mother's continued questions. She wished to hear the minutiae of their daily lives and to know for how long their Guards regiment, newly returned from Spain after tremendous success in the war, would be staying in London.

The dowager continued to guide the conversation on these topics for the rest of the afternoon and throughout dinner, without appearing to notice the repetitiveness of her questions. Leander was aware of a sense of relief when she was eventually persuaded to retire for the night, leaving the three alone in the drawing room.

"I've heard there are some good hells recently opened," Burnage started, his eyes shining with excitement.

Leander remained neutral. "Some new hells have opened, certainly. But unless you wish to lose your entire fortune with one throw of the dice, I suggest you avoid them."

"Oh, Lea." Henry punched his brother's arm affectionately. "You never used to be this dull. What's the problem? Don't tell me you've gamed away the family fortune."

Leander laughed briefly, a rather forced sound. If only it were so simple. No, he seemed to have forgotten how to enjoy himself. He couldn't see *how* to enjoy himself with Bella gone.

"Those hells are full of sharks and ivory turners," he said. Or so Jack had told him, disgust in his face as he had spoken of them.

Henry rose to his feet. "Well, in that case, you had best chaperone us."

Warmth blossomed inside Leander at the invitation, his prior misgivings about Henry's return dissipating.

The door of the residence in St James's Street was opened to them not by the expected footman but by a squat individual with a flattened nose. He looked as if he would be more at home in the prizefighting ring than the hallway of a London townhouse.

The three declared their names, and Leander was afforded a little private amusement that it was Captain Talbot and Captain Burnage whose admission appeared to be momentarily in question. He could not be sure if it was because they were not known for their fortune or if their regimentals militated against them. He had heard tales of young officers home from the war becoming too high-spirited and causing rather more damage than simply boxing the Watch. The prizefighter looked for guidance to a clerkish-looking fellow, who was seated at a small table covered with papers. His small nod confirmed they were all to be admitted.

The house was furnished in the first stare of elegance, but one thing marred its quiet gentility — a hubbub of gentlemen's voices, rising in volume as they ascended the stairs. The doors to a salon at the top of the stairs were open and gentlemen were crowded around a Hazard table in the centre of the room. The atmosphere was noisy, and Leander decided to continue exploring. The second salon he entered had an EO table, and the excited volume of the players, coupled with the noise from the wheel, drove him to a smaller, quieter chamber. This room held a Faro Bank along with groups of chairs and sofas arranged around the room. He presumed these were for gentlemen to recover from the excitement of the evening's play and to digest whatever supper the house provided.

Having somewhere lost Henry and Burnage — he guessed that they had been drawn to the game of Hazard with the inevitability of moths to a candle — he ventured into the quieter salon. He chose a seat from which he could claim he was watching the play, but his attention was not upon the cards. He never again wished to witness the realisation of ruin in a man's face after an ill-advised wager.

Glancing around the room, he noticed some acquaintances. He smiled briefly at George Fitzgerald when their eyes met and was disconcerted to see shock on Fitzgerald's face before he returned Leander's greeting. He was still watching as Fitzgerald dug his elbow into the side of the gentleman seated beside him and nodded his head, unmistakably indicating Leander. The other gentleman raised his quizzing glass and surveyed Leander. A look of amazement spread over his face before, perceiving that Leander was still observing them, he too greeted the earl.

Leander's lip curled slightly as he looked away, realising that he now possessed a reputation as a sober upright pillar of society. Not that he particularly wished to be associated with some of the wastrels who haunted these places, and he certainly had no interest in gambling large sums in an establishment where the bank always won, but he had somehow started to behave like a staid family man twice his age.

He sighed slightly. He had immersed himself in work and duty since Bella's death, but it was only now he understood how removed from his contemporaries he had become. Most faces here were unfamiliar to him. Take the character in the corner—a dark complexion, his dress rich but careless in a way that proclaimed he cared little for the opinion of society. Leander was certain he had never set eyes on him, though the deference with which his circle of friends was treating him indicated that he was a man of some standing. He took the opportunity to ask the servant who brought him a glass of champagne.

"His Grace the Duke of Arden, my lord," the man informed him.

The name was one with which Leander was familiar. It was a name with which all of London and some of the more enlightened provinces were familiar. Arden represented all that was decadent in the *ton*, his philandering ways extending far beyond opera dancers and actresses to ladies of quality. And it was not only widows or liaisons with married ladies, for it was said of him that he had ruined more than one young maiden. The number of duels that he had fought and won, the drunken orgies at which he presided, and his losses and gains at the gaming table had all assumed the proportions of legend. There were still darker things whispered about him. Only the coterie of wild young blades who formed his retinue knew the truth of these, but the intimations were there, and

Arden remained unrecognised by all save those wishing to court notoriety.

Leander became aware that Arden was returning his gaze, his heavy-lidded eyes holding what appeared to be a gleam of amusement. As Leander watched, Arden raised his glass in a mocking salute before putting it to his lips and tossing back the contents.

Perhaps it was the champagne, perhaps it was the shock of realising that his acquaintances now viewed him as a prig. Whatever the reason, some demon prompted Leander to his feet. In defiance of all proper behaviour, he crossed the room to Arden and introduced himself.

Those dark eyebrows raised briefly, a noble head was inclined, and one of the young men clustered around Arden was moving from his seat, offering it to Leander.

"So you're Ockley." The duke's aristocratic fingers curved elegantly around the stem of his glass and his dark eyes surveyed Leander as he sat. "I didn't think this to be your sort of place. I'd thought you more of a White's man."

The provocation was there. It was well known that Arden had been pre-emptively blackballed by the respectable club lest any member lose their faculties and propose him for membership.

"Indeed?" Leander said stiffly, his somewhat lamentable temper aroused by Arden's dismissal of him as a priggish bore. "And I thought you a legend, sir. A cautionary tale used by protective parents to keep young cubs in line."

Reaction rippled through the assembled ranks, but Leander's gaze was on Arden's face. A smile touched his lips as he looked at Leander. "A palpable hit, Ockley," he murmured. His voice was rich and soft, with a hint of steel that intrigued Leander.

"Lea." Henry's voice broke in. He was not precisely floored, but he was foxed enough to ignore all dictates of manners as he tugged insistently at his brother's arm. Knowing that if he resisted, Henry would only become more forceful, Leander allowed himself to be raised to his feet. His brother had been the same since nursery days—when he wanted something, he wanted it *now*, and it was usually attention he craved. Leander directed a small bow towards Arden, whose smile had widened at the spectacle Henry was making of them both, before following his brother's urgent strictures to leave immediately.

Henry pulled Leander down the staircase and out of the house, Burnage following close behind. Once on the street, away from the interested scrutiny of those gathered within, Leander swung round on his brother.

"What in God's name possessed you to behave in such a way?" he demanded, annoyed and embarrassed.

The anger in Henry's eyes was magnified by the amount of champagne he had drunk. "For God's sake, Lea—that was *Arden*." Fury and disgust filled his voice.

"And that is sufficient for you to make a fool of yourself, and of me?"

"How can you not know?" Henry was withering. "He is a devil of the worst kind—libidinous, dissolute, a libertine without a shred of decency, preying on men and women alike. Had you told me this is one of his haunts, I would never have agreed to come." His gaze flicked to Burnage before returning to Leander. "You judge us to need a chaperone, but *you* require a nursemaid."

Leander wrenched his arm out of his brother's tenacious hold. "Is that what you think of me? An innocent at large, unable to fend for myself?"

"Not precisely," Henry replied, rather unconvincingly. "But you haven't seen what Thomas and I have."

"That's true, Henry," Leander told him with deadly calm. "While you've been fighting to save this country from the threatened incursion of our enemies, I've been working to ensure there's a country worth returning to."

He thrust his brother from him and strode away, fuming. Hell and damnation, but his brother was as blinded by tales of his exploits as was their mother. He believed the stories with which she had filled his head as a child, reading the translations from the Greek that Leander's father had made. He thought himself to be living the part of some hero with a duty to save the lesser mortals around him.

That Henry loved a man was just another example of the pernicious influence of the ancient Greeks. Leander paused in his step. That wasn't fair. The truth was that Henry was scarcely alone in having a predisposition for those of his own sex. For some, such indulgence ceased when they left school, while for others it was a way of life, although most of the latter covered it with the facade of marriage.

The problem was that Henry and Burnage were not as careful as they should be. Leander's deepest fear remained that their mama would one day happen upon the two lovers the way he had done. Occasionally, he wondered why he was so concerned with protecting her from the knowledge of their vice. But then he upbraided himself. She had nothing else in her life, save a son who had signally failed to present her with the heir to the title she had every right to expect. He knew he had to marry again, but not yet. He would find a suitable well-bred woman in due course. No chit out of the schoolroom with fancies and romance in her head, but a woman who would understand about a marriage of convenience.

But not yet.

CHAPTER THREE

If Henry thought about what his brother had said to him that night, it was not evident from his subsequent behaviour. That was ever the way with Henry, Leander knew. If he didn't like what he heard, he ignored it. He continued to treat Leander with perfect civility and vague fondness, underlain with a hint of condescension that Leander could not be sure existed outside his imagination.

And truth to tell, while their mother's attentions to the guests drove Leander out of the house more often than was his wont, resulting in his purchase of both the bay and the restive grey hunter, he welcomed having male company over the dinner table. Of course his mother had invited several guests, all families with hopeful daughters, but her object was now seeing Henry wed. Leander was no doubt forgotten until Henry returned to Spain.

He took the opportunity of his mother having her other son's company to plan a visit to his estate. A recent letter from his steward, Mr Bartlett, had described the damage caused to the sawmill by a fire. Leander had written back immediately, noting his concern for the sawyer and his family. He had thanked Bartlett for ensuring their welfare in the aftermath of the blaze, but he wished to visit in person and reassure those who depended upon him that he was acquainted with their situation. He also wanted to consult with Bartlett about taking advantage of the unfortunate incident to bring forward his plans for developing the mill. He had an idea that the creek might be deepened to allow access to barges. That would facilitate increased sales of lumber, which would add to the estate's prosperity. Leander was still mentally drawing up and discarding different plans as he made arrangements to leave early on Tuesday morning.

On Monday evening, Henry and Burnage once more invited him to accompany them on their nightly indulgence. Leander welcomed the opportunity to stop thinking about barge draughts and was pleased by the prospect of a livelier evening than those he usually suffered. Not long after reaching Vauxhall Gardens, however, he found himself wishing he had not accepted the invitation. The affair, billed harmlessly enough as a masquerade, was little more than a wild romp. Both ladies and gentlemen seemed intent on taking advantage of the parlous anonymity provided by their masks to behave with no regard for decency.

Leander suffered the indecorous atmosphere for a time. His discovery that he was now viewed as a model of dull rectitude would not let him show his disapproval and leave. But after a couple of hours' unmitigated boredom, the delighted shrieking of one lady as her masked pursuer clutched her in his arms, his hand squeezing down the front of her dress to grope at her breasts, was too much for Leander. He despised vulgarity. His views were nothing to do with righteous attitudes and all to do with taste, he realised. There was a time and a place for the pleasures of the flesh, and this was neither. He glanced around for his companions, ready to make his excuses and leave.

There was no sign of Henry and Burnage. He did not care to venture into the groves or along the dark walks in search of them, for he was under no illusion as to the activities currently in progress therein. Wherever they were, he was certain they would be preoccupied with one another and hoped they would not lose all sense of caution in the dark night.

Ignoring pleas from the ladies of doubtful repute who had

been trying to gain his attention, Leander removed his mask and strode purposefully towards the Water Gate, whence he would take a boat to return him to more civilised surroundings. He would visit Caroline, the widow whose company he enjoyed on a regular basis. She would never be party to such a mockery of pleasure. She combined breeding and beauty with intelligence and taste. Theirs was an arrangement founded on mutual need and acceptance that romantic attachment between them was neither expected nor possible. He had sometimes thought he might marry her, had she not declared her aversion to enduring the restrictions of marriage again.

"Leaving already, Ockley?"

The figure before him was unmistakable, although the mask hid his features. He was slightly taller than Leander, with broad shoulders tapering to narrow hips and skin-tight pantaloons clinging to powerful thighs. His long dark hair was carelessly tied back in open contempt for fashion. This could be none other than the Duke of Arden. The voice, too, Leander recognised — like rich red wine but with that hint beneath of something darker and stronger. At that moment, Leander realised he must have partaken of the arrack punch more enthusiastically than he had intended.

"Duke." He bowed stiffly. He was not surprised to see him here. His presence confirmed Henry's telling of the man's character.

"Arden," the duke corrected him. Then that tone mocked again. "You disapprove. A little too immodest for you?"

Leander refused to be made to feel like a prig. "I find such brazenness tedious."

He could have sworn those dark eyebrows rose. "You prefer subtlety, do you, Ockley?"

"Yes," he said. "So if you will excuse me." He was annoyed to find Arden remained standing in the middle of the path, forcing Leander to walk around him.

"Off to visit your ladybird in Hertford Street?"

Leander swung round on his heel, his eyes quartering what could be seen of Arden's face. "What do you know of that?" he demanded.

Full lips rose in a lazy, mocking smile. "I like to do my research, Ockley." He inclined his head before he began to move away. "I trust you have a most . . . *enjoyable* evening."

Leander was left staring after him.

Leander left for Ockley the following morning, as planned. But as he rode over his land, as he worked with his steward and spoke to the sawyer, the memory of the duke's mocking smile kept returning to him. He had asked Caroline what she knew of Arden. She was aware of nothing more than general gossip. Her opinion of the man reflected Henry's attitude, if expressed a little less forthrightly.

Arden's knowledge worried him. Research, the man had said. For what purpose? Leander was no gamester. He gambled a little, as did all men, but no large sums. He drank to excess at times in the company of his friends but no more than others. He might have little patience for his brother, but that was scarcely a novelty in the world. None knew of his attachment to Caroline as he would not open her to idle gossip, but that apart, there was nothing with which he might be reproached and held to ransom. His life was a model of propriety — boredom, some might say. Leander would not have disagreed with that summation, but he was not one for mindless pleasure. He had tried once. Shortly after Bella's death, he had plunged into a short-lived whirl of drinking hard and spending his time with like-minded blades who had fair game in their — admittedly blurred — sights. His indulgence had brought him no relief, only guilt.

As he thought of Arden, Henry's words came back to him,

that Arden seduced innocents. Yet Leander's marriage to Bella had been one that fully celebrated the pleasures of the flesh, and now Caroline and he enjoyed their regular liaisons. He knew that he was no innocent for the plucking.

This conviction meant that when he encountered the Duke of Arden upon his return to town, he did not hesitate overlong before accepting the man's invitation to ride together. Indeed, he welcomed the diversion, for he had been hailed during his afternoon ride in the park by Lady Annesley. Comfortably established in her barouche, she appeared set to continue talking all afternoon of her daughter's accomplishments, regardless of Miss Westcourt's evident mortification as she sat silently beside her mother.

Leander was just calculating to himself when his new riding boots would be ready — following Jack's enthusiastic recommendation, he had tried a different man for the pair he wore today and was not completely satisfied with them — when he became aware that the good lady had stopped talking. That she was, in fact, stiffening in outrage.

"Lady Annesley?" Leander asked.

There was no answer. Leander turned to follow her indignant gaze and saw the Duke of Arden approaching, mounted on a mettlesome black horse. Drawing to a halt before them, Arden inclined his head to Lady Annesley in a way that managed to insult rather than compliment and ran his gaze over Miss Westcourt in an entirely improper manner. He sat his horse with easy grace, his reins gathered lazily in his right hand. The exquisite cut of his dark coat was evidently the work of a master. The white of his buckskins was displayed to advantage against the leather saddle, and the polish of his top boots matched that of Leander's own.

Arden tapped his whip slowly against his left boot as he considered Leander. "Ockley?" he invited.

A moment of madness assailed Leander. It was this or be condemned to hours of tedious company. He also felt that removing the man from Miss Westcourt's presence would be the proper thing to do. Taking his leave of the still speechless Lady Annesley, he turned his horse and accompanied Arden along the ride.

"Are you certain you can afford to be seen with me?" That lazy mocking drawl again, a sideways glance from brilliant dark eyes, while something that might have been amusement tugged at the corners of his mouth.

Leander kept his gaze between his horse's ears, though he was aware of the scandalised glances his companion was attracting. "I think my credit can bear it," he agreed blandly.

Silence fell, broken only by the sound of their horses' hooves on the tan. After a while, Leander glanced at his companion. "I don't recall seeing you ride in the park before."

The smile grew, and Arden turned in the saddle to face him. "You thought my physical activities to be conducted after dark?"

Leander's cheeks heated. It was what he had imagined, but he had not meant to imply so. "The inference is yours."

Arden laughed softly. "Oh come, Ockley, we both know how the *ton* love their simple narratives. Should you believe their tattle, I am beyond all hope of salvation, just as your heroic brother is held in higher regard even than Nelson."

Leander shot him a sharp look, then concentrated on making his horse step out. He knew his face gave away more than it should. The heel on the side away from Arden dug into his mount with sudden force. His action caused the animal to curvet protestingly, providing an excuse for Leander to turn his attention from Arden.

Arden watched in silence, but those heavy-lidded eyes missed nothing. Once Leander had brought his horse back under control, Arden remarked, "You have a good seat,

Ockley."

Without knowing why, Leander felt his cheeks heat once more. When he looked back at Arden, he saw the man was watching him with a curiously intent expression.

"Do you feel your credit sufficient to allow you to dine with me tonight?" Arden asked.

Leander hesitated. He had no intention of forming a friendship with someone who had as unsavoury a reputation as Arden. On the other hand, there was something about the man's shameless flouting of convention that he, brought up as a dutiful first-born son, found oddly alluring.

"Or would your brother disapprove?"

The question was murmured and blatantly manipulative, but it was enough for Leander to meet Arden's eyes and accept his invitation.

CHAPTER FOUR

Leander spent longer than usual dressing for his evening engagement. His valet, used to his master's simple tastes, was overjoyed to have his skills finally appreciated. Leander's navy swallow-tailed coat had a collar of plush velvet, his cravat was arranged in a perfect Waterfall, his waistcoat of white watered silk had been chosen only after due consideration, and his pantaloons clung tightly to his legs with no hint of a crease to mar them.

"Magnificent!" the dowager proclaimed on seeing him descend the stairs. And then the full meaning of his dress burst in upon her. "But why are you not attending Almack's?" she asked in disappointment. "Sophia will be there, you know."

Leander was puzzled until he recalled who Sophia was. "I'm engaged with friends elsewhere."

The dowager's beautiful face fell further. "Oh, *Leander!*" she wailed. "Unless you make a push, you will find she has been wed elsewhere while you have been shilly-shallying. Lord Ramsbottom is an assiduous suitor, and his fortune is quite respectable, though not as handsome as your own. He is of course only a viscount, and he has that horrid growth on his nose, but you cannot rely on young girls being constant in their affections if you will not give so much as a hint of your intentions. And how I will face dear Lady Annesley—"

He silenced her by raising her hand to his lips. "Good night, Mama," he said firmly, and left.

On being admitted to Arden's townhouse in Berkeley

Square, Leander was shown to the drawing room. It was more masculine than the one in Green Street. The maroon drapes, the dark gold Axminster carpet, and the Chinese wall coverings might have rendered the room too dark if not for its spacious proportions and the chandeliers reflected in large gilt-framed looking glasses. No musical instruments lurked, awaiting interminable performances by young ladies. Perhaps most welcome of all, there were no fresh flower arrangements liable to send an unwary guest into fits of sneezing. Leander suspected the ladies of his acquaintance would declare the effect oppressive, but he found it more welcoming than his own drawing room, which for the first time struck him as rather fussy.

As Arden came to greet him, his stride somehow both lazy and predatory, Leander stared for an instant. The man was immaculate in a way that declared the usual carelessness in his dress to be a choice he made. His claret coat was moulded across his broad shoulders and he had a fob at his waist, drawing the observer's eye inexorably to the close-fitting pantaloons he wore. His dark hair was still unmodishly long and tied back, but for the first time, Leander felt that this suited the man—a suggestion of wildness presently tamed, to be released when Arden so chose.

He blinked at the oddness of this fancy and returned Arden's greeting. Once Arden had ensured he was furnished with a glass of excellent burgundy, apparently laid down by the previous duke, Leander was introduced to the ten young men already present. He was familiar with their names, although he had only previously made the acquaintance of two of them, emphasising to him the different circles in which he and Arden moved.

They received him politely but were in the throes of a lively debate over the abilities of the latest prizefighters to emerge on the circuit. Arden drew Leander to one side. He sat—or rather sprawled — on a chaise longue upholstered in gold damask and indicated for Leander to take the Chesterfield beside him.

"What news of the war?" he asked.

Leander was surprised by the question. He was scarcely in a better position than anyone else to know. He had heard Henry's and Burnage's first-hand accounts, such as they were, but as the finer points of strategy were lost on the dowager, it was the domestic details of their life fighting the French that interested her. Leander had seen little of the two returned heroes other than at the dinner table and consequently had not learned a great deal.

"I know nothing more than may be gleaned from the newspapers," he said.

"But your brother is recently returned from the fighting," Arden pointed out.

Leander's rare smile dawned. "And I can tell you in absorbing detail of the inexplicable delays in paying the officers, the many challenges posed by bivouacking in peasants' abandoned huts, and the revolting nature of the food served at Headquarters. Other than that, I am none the wiser."

Arden laughed. "I thank you, but no. What, then, of your horses? I hear you had a recent victory at Newmarket."

And so the tone for the evening was set. Relaxed, sensible, masculine conversation, free-flowing alcohol, and congenial company. Leander was seated beside Arden at the table and enjoyed his undivided attention. The man had a breadth of knowledge that surprised Leander. His views on the *ton's* double standards were refreshingly frank and all was couched in the lazy mockery that so intrigued Leander. He could not be sure whether he was being laughed at, or with, and the uncertainty lent a particular interest to their exchanges.

At length, Arden appeared to recall his duty to his other

guests, and the party adjourned to the drawing room. A transformation had taken place during their absence. Tall candelabra stood at the back of the room, illuminating the chaise longue placed between them, with chairs and sofas arranged in a semi-circle facing this area. It looked like any other after-dinner entertainment that Leander was used to, except for the fact there was no harpsichord and no daughter of the house ready to impress the assembly with her interpretation of an unfortunate composer.

He became aware that no servants were present when Farquhar, the gentleman who had been seated opposite him during dinner, pressed a glass of wine into his hand.

Leander was beginning to feel uncertain about these developments. But as his host took the seat in the centre of the semi-circle and looked at him with invitation in his gaze, indicating the chair beside him, there was nothing Leander could do but join him. Arden leaned towards him, though not far enough. Leander had to bend close to catch what he said over the somewhat inebriated conversations taking place around them.

"A little *divertissement* for my friends." Arden's voice was smooth and soft, disconcertingly close to Leander's ear. "I find that digestion is aided by an increased flow of blood, don't you?"

There was that look again, the one that informed Leander that he was being mocked by a reference he did not understand. He murmured a platitude and sat back in his seat to await events. Moments later, a figure slipped through the folding doors from the next salon and stood before the assembled company. It was immediately apparent what type of *divertissement* Arden had in mind. The lady was blonde, with a figure that Leander thought the result of judicious padding of feminine garments — until she removed them.

When he was a very young man, Leander had gone with

friends to a brothel where out-of-work ladies of the stage earned their living and had paid for a show that pretended to emulate the one he now witnessed. The comparison to this was as cider to champagne. Leander took a deep draught from the glass in his hand and settled deeper into his seat to watch.

As the lady in question stripped off her final layer of clothing and moved her hands over her full breasts, Leander's cock announced its discomfort within his pantaloons. Leander attempted to ignore its message, instead watching speechlessly as the lady laid herself on her back on the chaise longue. She allowed her legs to fall open and what was revealed as a result to face her rapt audience as she ran her hands slowly and wantonly all over her body. They finally drifted up her inner thighs, caressing tantalisingly.

Leander was vaguely aware of the men around him, of their concentration on the scene before them, but his attention was focused on that hand. She stroked herself while her other hand continued to caress her breasts. Biting her lip, she moaned and tossed her head. Her pace started to increase, her cries became louder, and Leander shifted surreptitiously in his chair. The actresses on whom he had spent his money all those years ago had been a mockery. This woman, with her pliant limbs, her abandoned search for pleasure, right there in front of him, was unbelievably erotic. The fact she was doing this on the same piece of furniture he had seen Arden seated on only hours before somehow gave an added thrill to what he was seeing.

Leander was aware of Arden beside him, demonstrating no reaction to the show before him. His muscular legs were open, to be sure, but that was how he had sat down, a provocative sprawl. Everything he did contrived to provoke. Leander sat still, trying to ignore the increasing pressure against his pantaloons and to subdue the excitement he felt as he watched her stroking herself to completion only feet away from him. She finally, gaspingly, finished.

Arden leaned over to him as she left the room. "Tell me, Ockley, how does that compare to your usual after-dinner entertainments?"

Leander choked on a laugh as he thought of the previous evening's performance by an earnest bespectacled young lady in blue dimity. This parody was very deliberate, he realised.

"She had more aptitude than most after-dinner performers I've witnessed," he said.

A smile hovered around the corners of Arden's mouth. "Really?" he drawled. "Perhaps I should introduce you to a broader spread of talent."

An unaccustomed rush of wild exhilaration surged through Leander. He held Arden's gaze deliberately. "Perhaps you should."

An aristocratic eyebrow raised. Leander sensed that he had taken Arden by surprise and enjoyed the knowledge. In a deliberate echo of Arden's first gesture to him, he raised his glass to Arden before drinking deeply. Arden leaned closer still to Leander.

"You'd like to see more, would you, Ockley?" he offered, his voice low and caressing.

One corner of Leander's mouth lifted. "Why not?"

Arden beckoned to one of his other guests and murmured something into his ear. The man disappeared through the doors used by the lady. For an instant, Leander wondered if he had taken leave of his senses, goading Arden in such a way. But as Arden turned back to him and dark eyes held his, he regretted nothing.

CHAPTER FIVE

Leander rose later than usual the following day. He had not gained his bed until the sky over the city was beginning to lighten. He awoke to the accusing silence of his valet, who was gathering up from the dressing room floor the crumpled clothes that Leander had let fall. Unwilling to face his reproach, Leander decided to keep to his bed until Morris had finished and left him in peace. He lay there, thinking about the previous night.

Arden had taken him at his word and shown him more. Leander swallowed slightly as he remembered. His desire to surprise Arden had led him into a declaration that was foolhardy, to say the very least. As soon as the next performers entered the room, Leander had known he'd made a grievous misjudgement. His instinct had prompted him to leave. He was scarcely a puritan, but this was far outside the bounds of acceptable behaviour, even among a party of bloods such as this. But as this was in direct response to his request, he could hardly walk away from it. Instead, he sought refuge in his wine glass, which Farquhar had kept refilling, waiting for everything to be over. The display was inappropriate, to say the least. Improper, certainly. And exciting . . .

Leander threw back the bedclothes and swung round to sit on the edge of his bed. Damnation. He'd been forced to sit in company and watch a man and a woman having intimate relations and found to his horror that he had become aroused. As he'd watched them, as he'd heard their passion, he had been sore with need. For a moment he'd thought of Bella. For an even briefer instant, of Caroline. His relations with them had always been pleasurable, but the sounds of delight and abandonment from the couple before him had been new to him.

After what had seemed an interminable time, during which the two figures on the makeshift stage pleasured one another in any number of different ways, the man stood while the woman knelt before him and slid her mouth down onto his cock. She was careful to show the assembled audience every step of what was occurring for their pleasure. As he'd watched, Leander's hand had moved very casually from the arm of his chair to his lap, brushing against where his cock was pushing against his pantaloons. He'd swallowed hard and concentrated on his peripheral vision to see whether anybody had noticed. What he'd seen had stopped him dead.

Young Farraday, Lord Linton's youngest son, had been leaning back in his chair, his eyes half-closed as he watched the act unfolding before him. Sir Richard Hazell, seated beside him, was stroking Farraday's cock through his pantaloons. As Leander watched from the corner of his eye, he had seen Hazell begin to unfasten them. His cheeks hot, Leander had jerked his attention back to the scene before him.

That hadn't helped him. The man had been thrusting into the woman's mouth, and the sight, together with the soft moans from Farraday's direction, had proved too much for Leander. His hand in his lap had moved so that his wrist rubbed against the hardness of his cock through soft, clinging material. He'd had to bite his lip to prevent a sound from escaping him. That was when Arden had leaned across to him, his mouth close to Leander's ear to ensure his low voice wouldn't disturb anyone.

"They're rather accomplished, don't you think?"

Leander had jumped, guiltily. Instantly stilling his hand, he'd tried to match Arden's tone. "I suppose so," he'd admitted, his throat dry.

"With a little more practise, I might invite them to entertain us formally."

Leander had turned to face Arden, his brow furrowed in confusion. Arden had indicated with his eyes past Leander, back towards the gentlemen he'd been trying so hard to ignore. Leander twisted to follow his gaze, and Arden's meaning became clear. Hazell was now kneeling beside Farraday's seat. Farraday's erection was protruding from his open pantaloons and Hazell's hand closed around it with an expertise that had Farraday crying out, his head falling back and his eyes closing. Farraday raised his hips to thrust into Hazell's hand, and as he did so, Hazell took the opportunity to work Farraday's pantaloons down around his thighs. As soon as he'd realised what he was seeing, Leander had turned abruptly away.

"What do you think, Ockley?" Arden had spoken again. "Do you find them inspiring?"

Leander had paused for an instant, his attention on not flaring up at the smoothly spoken man beside him, mocking him. Or so he had thought. As he'd glanced at Arden, Arden's eyes had shown no mockery but a keen interest in his answer.

"I venture their enthusiasm compensates for any lack of technique," he had managed at last.

Arden had smiled, as though satisfied about something. "Good," he'd murmured.

With that, he had turned his attention back to the show before them. Leander sat mechanically watching, but it was now the sounds from his right that had held his attention, the soft groans and pleadings. He'd flicked one more glance sideways and seen Farraday alternately thrusting up into Hazell's hand and then pushing down on his other hand, sounds of need and desire escaping him. Leander had quickly looked away again, only to find the couple on the stage reaching the climax

31

of their show in parallel with the others. As Farraday's moans became sobbing sounds, he'd found himself incapable of not looking back at him. He watched as the man writhed on the fingers inside him and came in Hazell's practised hand, his seed spurting over his clothing.

Leander turned away to find the couple in front of them had also finished. He'd sat still, uncomfortably aware that his excitement was closely outlined by his tight pantaloons. When Arden had risen to his feet, however, he'd had to follow suit. He had found to his relief that, as the chairs were rearranged and casual conversations resumed, his plight slowly eased.

Arden had once more appropriated him. Leander was aware that Arden was neglecting his duty towards his other guests, but his inattention did not appear to cause offence. Neither did Farraday and Hazell's sudden disappearance. And Leander was enjoying Arden's company too much to surrender it voluntarily. Arden intrigued Leander. Despite spending hours in conversation with him, he could not claim to have any idea of the man's true character. He did, however, find Arden's intelligence and dry sense of humour stimulating.

When the time came for Leander to depart, Arden had wished to have the pleasure of his company again soon. Social niceties were of course being observed, but there was a look in his eyes that convinced Leander he meant it.

Leander rasped a hand over his unshaven chin and decided to arise for the day. His mother had requested his company at another social gathering that evening and Leander hoped her friend Lady Linton would not be present. He wasn't sure he could face her, with the memory of her beloved son's shameless public display so fresh in his mind.

An evening of unrelieved boredom was lightened slightly

by the appearance of Henry and Burnage. They brought some life to the party, some physical masculinity amidst all the talk of fashion and the latest *on-dits*. The three were in demand as suitable partners for the dancing, and, for once, the scarlet coats failed to carry the day with the ladies. From conversation he could not help overhearing, Leander gleaned that all the young ladies present knew how Sophia Westcourt, the Season's most notable Beauty, cast covetous eyes on the Earl of Ockley. For reasons that were to him unfathomable, this made his title and fortune even more desirable.

When Leander finally managed to break free from the determined attempts of matchmaking mamas and a hostess who was insistent that no young lady should go home from her ball without having danced with at least one gentleman, he assured his retreat by making his way outside. The terrace was cooler than the stifling ballroom, although almost its equal in brightness, lit as it was by strings of colourful lanterns.

He leaned against the stone balustrade, staring into the darkness of the gardens. Last night had thrown into sharp relief the emptiness of the life he was forced to lead. There, he had been able to speak his mind and, almost paradoxically, also delight in the verbal fencing that Arden enjoyed. Here, there was nothing save being charming and drawing out yet another young lady who could scarcely bring herself to raise her eyes from his waistcoat or, if she were a different type of young lady, to stop staring into his face. His one consolation was that Henry and Burnage had been engaged for as many dances as he had to suffer.

"Leander!"

Stifling an undutiful groan, he turned to see his mother approaching along the terrace, her gown of primrose lustring shining in the light from the lanterns and her fair hair partially covered by a dowager's cap that did nothing to diminish her beauty. His smile held genuine warmth by the time she reached him.

"Leander," she remonstrated with him. "Sophia is in a fit of the sullens because you have only danced with her once. And I understand they are Lord Ramsbottom's flowers she wears tonight, not yours. Is your intention to let her slip through your fingers to that upstart?"

Leander suppressed a laugh at that unlikely description of a member of a family equal in age, if not distinction, to the Talbots. He neglected to inform his mother that Sophia Westcourt did not wear his flowers primarily because he had not sent her any. He did, however, attempt to lay her indignation to rest. "Do you wish me to cause talk about Miss Westcourt by engaging her to dance with me again? I have stood up with no other lady more than once. To so single her out would cause comment."

"It would please her," his mother returned sharply.

"Mama, the sooner you accept the fact that I have no interest in Sophia Westcourt, the happier you will be."

His parent changed tack. Standing close to him, she raised her face to his. "You do understand that I want only the best for you, for you to be happy again."

He sighed. "I know."

"And Sophia is a lovely girl. Oh, she has the Westcourt name of course, and her fortune—did I mention that?—but she's a delightful child. I feel sure you two will be perfectly happy together if only you will rid yourself of this foolish notion that you have no interest in her."

Goaded, Leander replied with impatient honesty. "Don't you see, Mama, you've said it yourself. She's a child. She'll be looking for excitement, romance, and love." Leander held his mother's gaze for an instant before adding softly, "I can offer her nothing save my name."

Tears shone in the dowager's eyes. "Oh, Leander, don't

you understand? If you allow yourself to be moped forever over dear Isabella, you'll never remarry. Do you think that's what she would want for you?"

He turned away sharply to hide the anger in his face. As if she had really known Bella and what she had wanted.

"I'll think about it, Mama," he told her abruptly. "But it won't be Sophia Westcourt."

He'd already seen the look in the girl's eyes that told him she was halfway to being in love with him, the tragic earl, widowed so young. To encourage her would be to court disaster.

CHAPTER SIX

After the tedious evening he had been obliged to suffer, Leander felt a need for relaxed conversation and agreeable company. He was frustrated to find Caroline was not at home. Walking back to Green Street, disappointed in his quest, he acknowledged ruefully that conversation and company were not all he felt the need for. Unbidden images had visited his dreams the previous night. Although he could not remember them, he knew they were related to the scenes he'd witnessed in Arden's drawing room.

Recently, he had come to realise that his liaisons with Caroline, while undoubtedly enjoyable, were a pleasantly satisfying habit more than anything else. For her too, he felt. What he'd witnessed under Arden's aegis had led him to wonder. The performance had been many things but was as far from merely pleasant or a simple release as he could imagine.

A voice close to his ear roused him from his reverie. "I find you abominably rude, Ockley."

He spun round to find Arden beside him, amusement in his face belying his statement.

"Not only have you sent away two of your most ardent female admirers with despair in their hearts, determined to wear the willow for you as you no longer have any tender feelings for them, but you blatantly ignore my attempt to attract your attention."

Confused, Leander looked past the duke and saw Lady Emilia and Lady Charlotte Beaumont walking away from him, backs held rather rigidly.

He returned his gaze to Arden, whose concentration did not seem to have wavered from Leander's face.

"It seems to me that such execrable manners demand a forfeit."

Leander raised an enquiring eyebrow. "And what might that be?"

Arden's head tipped thoughtfully to one side as he surveyed Leander. "I haven't yet decided. I think the first part will be to dine with me again tomorrow."

Leander hesitated.

"Unless you are otherwise engaged, of course," Arden added.

"I should be delighted to join you," Leander said swiftly. Tomorrow would be another assembly, another night of slow suffocation, stifling everything he was. It would do Henry no harm to escort their mother for once. Leander smiled at the thought and met Arden's eyes. That sudden spurt of elation ran through him again, leading him to the certain knowledge that, even if Henry had been unable to escort their mama, Leander would still have withdrawn from the engagement.

Arden inclined his head, his gaze holding Leander's. "I shall see you tomorrow then, Ockley," he said, before turning to cross the street.

Leander strode home with renewed vigour. At last, he had something to look forward to.

"Lea."

Leander looked up from his desk, where he had been working on instructions for Bartlett. He had decided to consult a surveyor about the advisability of dredging the creek and wished Bartlett to ensure the sawyer, Tom Grant, was provided with alternative work. It might be some time before a mill was once more fully functional on the estate.

"What is it, Henry?"

His brother looked unusually diffident as he entered the book room. "Are you busy?"

Leander laid down his quill, wondering what this was all about. "Not particularly."

"Oh, good." Henry regained his normal cheery composure and flung himself into a chair.

"Well?" Leander encouraged when nothing further was forthcoming.

Henry grimaced apologetically. "It's Mama, you know," he said. "Wants me to talk to you about the succession and so on."

Leander snorted. "*You* talk about siring heirs? Come on, Henry, face reality before they remove you to Bedlam."

There was a flash of resentment on Henry's face. "I'm not the earl," he muttered. "I don't have a duty to the name. And anyway, I don't like women—you do," he added ingenuously.

As Leander stared speechlessly at him, Henry shifted in his seat and met his brother's gaze with a dazzling smile. "Come on, Lea," he coaxed. "What's the harm in gaining a wife? Means you can roll around in bed with a female whenever you like without having to make arrangements first. With your title, you can have your pick—you don't have to settle for some antidote. I don't see what the problem is."

"And I don't understand what your sudden interest is." Leander's words were clipped.

"Oh yes, you do," his brother informed him with devastating honesty. "The longer you go without producing any offspring, the more pressure Mama puts on me to beget some, just to make sure. This way, Thomas and I are left in peace."

Leander was on his feet, so lightheaded his surroundings felt unreal. "It may have escaped your notice, brother, but my wife has been dead not yet two years, and you're telling me to go and find another one as if nothing had happened?" He broke off, breathing fast.

Henry stood up slowly, concern on his face. "Lea?"

Leander turned away. He knew the expression on his face must be raw. He could usually conceal his feelings more successfully than this, but Henry's clumsy words had taken him by surprise.

Henry reached out a hand and touched his brother's arm. "I didn't realise you still missed Bella."

"Still?" Leander laughed briefly, a sound that had little to do with humour. "She was the only woman I've ever loved, Henry. I know my duty, believe me, but I need more time." He turned to look into his brother's face. "I know she's dead. I don't mourn her any longer. But can you imagine what it will be like to have someone else take her title? To have them order the house as they choose, to have someone else's portrait hanging in the hall? To have Bella relegated to a dusty memory, yet one that is always scorned or diminished because they know I loved her?"

Henry's face was unwontedly sober. "I'm sorry. I suppose, if I lost Thomas . . ." His voice trailed off, his eyes bleak, and then he shook his head. "I'll deal with Mama," he said firmly.

Leander never found out what dealing with Mama entailed, but when he next encountered her, he swiftly became aware Henry must have spoken to her. She said nothing but took his hand and pressed it meaningfully, her eyes fixed speakingly on his face and a tremulous smile on her lips. More disconcertingly, when the conversation over dinner that evening turned to a discussion of the Beaumonts' upcoming rout, the dowager mentioned that Lord and Lady Annesley and their daughter would be attending without once commenting on the daughter's attractions. The brothers' eyes met across the table in a silent message.

Their amity was rudely shattered once the dowager had

retired from the table. Over port and snuff, Henry objected strenuously when informed by his brother that he would have to accompany their mother to the Beaumonts' the following evening.

"Why can't *you* do it? You said you would." Henry's face was resentful. "I did my bit at that ball the other night, doing the dutiful to all the old tabbies for Mama's sake. What can be so important you won't honour your word?"

"A dinner invitation that I wish to accept," Leander said. "And I thought, with you home, you might see your way to spending a little time with Mama." He tried a smile at Henry. "You know she would love you to escort her."

An answering smile lit Henry's face for an instant, before disappointment set in again. "But it will be an entire evening," he protested. "Even if you can procure an invitation for Thomas" — the lure with which Leander was trying to tempt his brother — "we'll scarcely be able to spend any time together."

Leander was unsympathetic. "You have all day every day together. I assume you have an arrangement unknown to the household for the nights. What's the sacrifice in one evening to make Mama happy?"

Eventually, with encouragement from Burnage, who looked uncomfortable at being caught in the midst of the brothers' quarrel, Henry conceded. "But I won't do it again," he threatened Leander.

"Nor should you have to," Leander agreed. While discussing who should sacrifice their evening to escort their parent to yet another mindless gathering, a thought had struck him. "Henry," he said slowly. His brother looked at him, suspicion writ large on his countenance. "What if we were to get Mama yoked? Then neither of us need go to those cursed things."

Henry's jaw dropped. "*Mama?*" he echoed blankly. "But she's — No, damn it, Lea, she can't marry again. She's our mother."

Leander was too taken with his idea to pay much heed to his brother's protest. "Sir John Gillingham has always been one of her admirers. He's a decent sort, reasonable fortune, and his wife died four years ago. Think about it, Henry," he urged his brother. "What will she do with herself once you've returned to Spain and if she succeeds in leg-shackling me to some heiress? Don't you think, as dutiful sons, we should encourage her to find happiness for herself?"

"You mean for *me* to encourage her, don't you?" Henry was blunt.

"You know she doesn't listen to a thing I say," Leander said. "The alternative, of course, is to spend your next leave abroad so you don't have to face this unending round of balls and soirées."

A look of horror crossed Henry's face. "What, spend my leave among foreigners? Damn it, Lea, I won't do it! Who is this fellow? Will he be there tomorrow, do you think?"

By the time the gentlemen joined the dowager in the drawing room, Henry was acquainted with everything Leander knew of Sir John. He also wore a look of grim determination, as if he were about to engage in a Forlorn Hope rather than play matchmaker at some society gathering. Leander had little faith in Henry's subtlety but every trust in his relentlessness. He was glad to leave the matter in his brother's hands so he might concentrate on enjoying another pleasurable evening with Arden.

As he once again trod up the steps to the door of the house in Berkeley Square, Leander was agreeably anticipating the evening to come. He did not know if there would be a repeat of the previous scandalous entertainment—he found himself hoping simultaneously both that there would and would not be—but he was looking forward to an evening of Arden's company.

He spent an instant at the looking glass in the hall to ensure his neckcloth bore no unintended creases and his hair looked as windswept as the style he favoured demanded, before following the butler to the drawing room. On being admitted, he was surprised to find he was the only guest present. Arden was reclining on a chaise longue — the one from the performance, Leander realised with shock — and gestured to the butler to provide his guest with a drink.

"I don't stand on ceremony with my friends," he informed Leander. "Have a seat."

Leander did as he was bidden, settling himself comfortably in a leather Chesterfield close enough to Arden to allow easy conversation.

"I'm surprised you're not engaged to the Beaumonts tonight," Arden observed idly. "I have a suspicion they have you in their sights for their eldest daughter."

"If you know that, you shouldn't be surprised that I'm not there."

Arden's eyes gleamed in acknowledgement of Leander's statement. He remained silent for a while, watching his guest. Leander sat at his ease, sipping his sherry and contrasting this civilised atmosphere to the overcrowded tedium that the Beaumonts' rout would no doubt become.

"Do you have any other guests tonight?" he asked Arden.

Arden's lips curved. "Not unless you wish it." He shifted slightly on the chaise longue, in a way that brought back vividly the images of Leander's last visit.

As Leander observed Arden's powerful legs sprawled in casual possessive ownership of the furniture, he remembered the last pair of legs he'd seen spread wantonly over it. He had the suspicion that his colour was raised as he looked back at Arden's face. "I had meant, any of your friends," he explained.

Arden shook his head slowly, holding Leander's gaze. "I hoped we might improve our acquaintance."

Leander was caught between the swift uprush of elation that he was beginning to feel more and more often in Arden's presence and a sudden very peculiar feeling such as he imagined a fly might feel, caught upon a web. Shaking his head slightly, he rapidly dispelled the illusion. There was no conceivable reason for his odd fancy unless it was too much sherry on an empty stomach. His host laughed suddenly and encouraged Leander to tell him more about the exceptional cattle he had heard the earl kept in his stables. With relief, Leander plunged into an enthusiastic and often heated discussion with Arden about horseflesh.

By the time dinner had ended, Leander found himself invited to join a party Arden would be hosting at his country seat the following week. Even in this he was flouting convention, by holding such a thing during the Season. The idea appealed to Leander, offering a retreat from the tedium of the *ton*. Arden had added that he wished Leander to join him at his manor in Quorn country later in the year, for he had admired the way Leander sat his horse and wished to have the opportunity to see him in action.

Leander had accepted both invitations, although he was sensible that he was unable to reciprocate. To think of presenting a man of Arden's reputation to his mother was inconceivable. He could only hope that Henry was making headway with the Sir John Gillingham venture and that the dowager would soon occupy her own place of residence.

"I beg your pardon?" Leander came back to the present, realising his host was awaiting an answer from him.

"I wondered, my dear Lord Ockley, if we might adjourn?" The exaggerated politeness, in sharp contrast to their relaxed conversation throughout the meal, indicated that he had repeated the question at least once.

Leander grinned unrepentantly and stood. "By all means, Your Grace." He bowed. "As Your Grace desires."

The room spun a little as he straightened up. It seemed the number of different wines they had sampled with each course had not been a wise idea. Or perhaps it had not been the number of wines but the amount of each that caused the problem. Arden was a generous host, and there was no doubt that, under his encouragement, his guest had been dipping deep. Fighting the urge to grin like a village idiot, a decidedly bosky Leander accompanied Arden back to the drawing room where they continued their lazy conversation and steady inroads on as smooth a port as Leander had ever tasted.

At some point in the small hours, Leander rose to take his leave. He successfully navigated his way downstairs despite the revolutions of the walls around him, but the cool air through the open front door was his undoing. Grabbing the doorframe, he breathed deeply, trying to bring the flight of steps before him into full focus. His blurred vision informed him that his footman appeared to be starting towards him.

An amused voice sounded in his ear. "Allow me to lend you my assistance, Ockley," and his arm was taken in a reassuringly firm grasp. He was vaguely aware of Arden waving away the footman and then a steady arm around him was helping him to his carriage. He clutched at the doorway, blindly feeling for the steps. Strong hands were on his waist, steadying him as he swayed up them before he collapsed into the seat. The carriage was suddenly full as Arden followed him in, propping him in the corner and straightening his legs. "Just as well your coachman knows where you live, Leander."

Leander's eyes blinked open again and he looked up into Arden's teasing gaze. A semblance of manners presented itself to him. "Pleasant evening. Thank you," he uttered thickly.

The hands paused on his legs as Arden smiled at him. "Sleep well, Leander."

Then Arden was gone, and the carriage was cold and empty without his company, his lazy drawl and his touch. Leander's eyes closed.

CHAPTER SEVEN

Leander was somewhat delicate when he emerged from his bedchamber the following afternoon. He found that his brother and Burnage were out and his mama was resting in preparation for the evening's exertions. Left to roam an empty house, he longed suddenly for company. He did not feel it appropriate to pay a call on Jack. If he and his bride were still negotiating their marriage, he would not thank Leander for interrupting them. His acquaintances at White's were simply that, acquaintances, and damned boring, most of them. He could always visit Angelo's academy and enjoy a bout with the fencing master, but the pounding in his head dissuaded him from doing so. He sent instead for one of his horses, hoping fresh air would clear his head.

By the time Leander reached the park, he was beginning to feel more the thing, having purposely chosen a smooth-actioned beast for his mount. His headache was slowly dissipating in the dampness of the overcast day, and he was able to greet acquaintances among the crowds thronging the park with an almost convincing display of good health. When he saw a familiar figure ahead of him on the ride, he forgot all about the residual pain in his head.

Before he could urge his horse forward, an autocratic voice claimed his attention. He turned reluctantly to find Lady Beaumont hailing him from the landau in which she and her daughters were ensconced.

"Why, Lord Ockley, I confess we have not seen you in what seems like an age — or so my daughters tell me," she declared playfully.

Lady Emilia hung her head, blushing in a not unbecoming manner and murmuring "Mama!" Lady Charlotte was made of sterner stuff and held Leander's gaze with a world of meaning in her deceptively innocent grey stare. Leander looked away to find Lady Charlotte's mama not at all discomposed by the forward behaviour of her second daughter.

"Delighted to see you Lady Beaumont, Ladies." Leander bowed slightly and would have urged his horse on had not the determined lady continued obliviously.

"Oh, but you have not yet told us if you will be attending the Lennoxes' ball on Saturday."

Leander cast a despairing glance at Arden's steadily retreating figure, and his eyes narrowed. Sir Richard Hazell, mounted on one of his infamously ill-broken youngsters, had joined Arden. They were walking their horses side by side, talking.

With difficulty, Leander pulled his attention back to the lady before him.

" . . . his wonderful deeds in Spain?" She was looking expectantly at him.

"Henry?" He made a shrewd guess, and then an idea occurred to him. He smiled at all three ladies as he warmly invited them to wait upon his mama the following day, when he knew that Captain Talbot and his good friend Captain Burnage would be present and delighted to entertain them with suitably dashing tales of heroism.

"May I ask, will *you* be there, my lord?" The coy glance might have worked from one of her daughters, but from this redoubtable matron, the effect was remarkably akin to having a tooth pulled.

"I regret that I have another appointment." He inclined his head courteously. "Ladies," he said, and left before any further entanglements could be attempted.

His immediate impulse was to ride after Arden and Hazell and join them, but as he saw their figures ahead of him, he hesitated. Arden was leaning towards the other man, his gaze fixed on his face. Hazell was chatting animatedly, his body inclined towards Arden in a way that irritated Leander. He abruptly swung his horse around and decided to return home. The excursion had somehow lost all pleasure for him.

Leander had not long returned to the house when he decided to call upon Caroline. He had paid her two visits since the first time he had dined with Arden, and on neither occasion had she been at home to visitors. His luck was no better on this occasion. If anything, the news he received sank his spirits further.

"Mrs Howarth is gone out of town, my lord," her butler informed him.

Leander concealed his surprise at the news. Caroline would not usually do such a thing without informing him. "When do you expect Mrs Howarth's return?"

"I really couldn't say, my lord."

That was as far as the man would be drawn. Dissatisfied, Leander had to admit defeat and retire. Caroline's recent absences, even before this unwelcome news, had occurred at the worst possible time, for he had not known since the days of courting Bella such desire as now seemed to consume him. He had become accustomed to stroking his cock, bringing himself to lonely release each night. And morning. And whenever else he could be sure of privacy. Perhaps all he needed was a week or so in the country with like-minded company, engaging in physical pursuits that would leave him exhausted and ready for sleep each night. It was boredom that currently led all his excess energy to be focused in his cock, that was all.

Leander was out of sorts that evening, unsettled by the unsatisfactory day he had spent. He retired to his book room to work on estate matters, finding sanctuary in the peaceful room where none but he ever spent much time. He was working through Bartlett's latest missive when there was the most cursory of knocks and the door opened.

"Lea," Henry said, as he strode into the room. His intrusion into Leander's haven somehow brought with it the uncertain nature of the world outside.

"What is it, Henry? I'm busy." Leander knew he was being ungracious but could not bring himself to care overmuch.

"I beg your pardon for disturbing you, but I wish most particularly to speak to you this evening," Henry said.

The level of politeness in his brother's words alerted Leander that this was no random visitation. Laying aside the quill with which he had been making annotations on Bartlett's closely written sheets, he gestured to a chair. It did not escape his notice that Henry had closed the door behind him. He couldn't be certain if it was to ensure they were not disturbed or to prevent Leander from escaping.

Henry settled himself in one of the chairs, then seemed not to know what to do next. He began perusing the spines of books through the glass doors of the bookcase beside him.

"Well?" Leander asked, when the silence had gone on a little too long.

Henry stopped chewing his lip, something Leander had never before seen him do and which warned him that whatever was forthcoming was liable to be an awkward subject. "The thing is, I've been thinking about what you said concerning Bella and not wishing her to be replaced," he said at last. "It occurred to me that if you were to wed a young girl, one who is entirely biddable, then that needn't be a concern. You could tell them how to go on and they would do so without question. Of course, your wife would have to obey you in any case, but you know how difficult some ladies can be when they set their mind to it. Start 'em early enough, and they won't know any different."

Leander was still attempting to understand why Henry was being so helpful all of a sudden when his brother continued more confidently. "I know you ain't ready to marry again yet, but when do you think you might be? If you give Annesley a hint, I expect he'll wait until the end of the Season."

Exasperated by Henry's lack of sensitivity, Leander bit down his rising temper because Henry's expression was earnest. His brother was attempting to help by meeting the objections Leander had set out. It was just that he had already forgotten the brief understanding he had reached of the emotions behind them.

"We have had this discussion already," Leander said. "My mind has not changed since a few days ago. I thought you understood that I am not ready to wed, so why raise the subject again?"

"I can see you ain't happy with me, Lea," Henry said. "But you've changed. You're a miserable fellow now, no pleasure to be had in anything, and I don't like to see it. Mama and I are agreed that a wife would be just the thing for you—cheer you up, make you sociable once more."

Leander closed his eyes briefly. It was either that or risk his fist connecting with his well-meaning but blockheaded brother's jaw.

"A wife would be just the thing for your happiness," Henry pushed.

"And yours?" Leander suggested. "For it would remove the most immediate pressure from you."

Henry gave a scapegrace grin, the one that earned him immediate forgiveness from ladies and gentlemen alike. "True," he owned. "Mama is all but flinging young ladies into my arms. It's most nerve-racking. She wishes me to have brats to inherit in case you slip your wind."

Despite everything, Leander's lips lifted in unwanted

humour. "Your concern at the prospect of my demise is touching, brother."

He was treated to another of Henry's grins. "We both know it ain't going to happen, but you must agree she's not wrong about needing an heir. Why don't you play the pretty with the Westcourt chit at the Lennoxes? Send her your flowers to wear, compliment her dress, you know how it goes. With your title and fortune, I wager she'll wait until you are ready, providing the offer is made."

He was as relentless as their mother and, for the first time, Leander felt sympathy for the French army. "It grieves me to cast a rub in the way of your plans for my future, but I shall not attend the Lennoxes' ball," Leander said firmly. "I am going into the country for a time."

Henry's brows drew down. "At this season? Not the estate again? Devil take it, Lea, you're becoming a damned bucolic!"

"Not the estate this time. With friends." Leander reached toward his quill, hoping that Henry would take his cue.

"Who?" Henry was pugnacious.

"Not that it is any of your concern, but if you must know, I am visiting Arden."

"*Arden?*" A tide of crimson swept up Henry's face. "What the devil do you think you're doing? I've told you, he is a vicious libertine, with a vileness of the very worst kind. You cannot—you *must* not continue this connection, for if you do, no one will receive you. And it's your duty, damn it—you must wed again and beget an heir. You can't shirk it. I won't—"

"You won't be forced into an unpleasant duty, is that it, Henry? Not when you can force me into one instead?" Leander's voice was edged with fury. "I will not be forced into *anything* by you, Mama, or anyone else. Do you understand me?"

"You have no idea of the true nature of the man," Henry

said stubbornly. "He is only casting out lures to you because of me. You—"

"*Out!*" Leander snarled, propelling himself from his chair and wrenching the door open. "Get out, Henry. I will not hear another word."

With one last fulminating glare, Henry stormed out.

Closing the door, Leander leaned his forehead against the wood, still holding onto the handle as he breathed heavily, trying to control his anger. The worst of it was that he knew Henry was right—that it *was* his duty. But not yet.

He eventually returned to his seat at the desk and stared blindly down at his papers before cursing and thrusting his chair back. He would give anything to hear Arden's lazy drawl consigning all paperwork to perdition. The thought that in two days' time he would have that opportunity steadied him slightly. Summoning a footman to bring him some wine, he stood staring into the fireplace, contemplating his escape.

CHAPTER EIGHT

Leander immured himself in the book room the following day, working once more on Bartlett's letter. He was not purposely avoiding his brother, but he was glad not to encounter him—he did not think he could bring himself to be civil to Henry. When finally he could find no more estate business with which to occupy his time, he selected at random one of his father's books. In reading of Etruscan vases, he lost all awareness of the modern world.

Many hours later, Pickett tactfully prised him from his haven. He was evidently acting on the dowager's orders, for she wished Leander to escort her to the Sedgewicks' assembly. They were hosting another glittering party in their determination to see both daughters wed this Season. So determined were they that they had invited every bachelor of the *ton*.

The result was a sad crush, the very sort that the dowager decried as being the most tedious of evenings yet one that she would not miss for the world. Leander gritted his teeth and prepared himself for a long night. The one redeeming feature was his knowledge that, once this was over, only one day remained before he became Arden's guest.

It was still early when Leander, his head bent to catch the pearls of wisdom dropping from the lips of the young lady with whom he had just been dancing, caught a glimpse of something from the corner of his eye. Something that had his head raising and his polite smile becoming genuine when he realised it was indeed Arden's figure he had seen. The young lady seemed somewhat breathless when he turned that smile upon her. She attempted to continue their conversation, but Leander was even more determined than she. He excused himself and threaded his way through the throng at the edge of the ballroom, keeping his prize in sight as he exchanged greetings with those he passed.

His concentration upon his goal meant that when his sleeve was grasped, it took him an instant to realise it was his mama.

"Leander," she whispered urgently. "This is your chance. That dreadful man, the Duke of Arden, is here and forcing his attentions upon Sophia. He did not even have an introduction! Rescue the poor child and she and her family will be forever grateful to you. Lord Ramsbottom has already made an attempt, but Arden is so shameless, he would not yield. Do something!"

It was a challenge to which Leander rose nobly. He advanced towards Arden, who was dressed in a black coat, a waistcoat of cream brocaded silk, and black silk knee breeches. He saw the sparkle in Miss Westcourt's deep blue eyes as she gazed up at Arden's face and knew that Arden was exerting himself to be as charming as only he knew how. She looked particularly fetching tonight, Leander conceded. Her three-quarter dress of sarsnet worn over an underdress of ivory satin was breathtaking on her elegant young figure, the modest pearl drops from her ears speaking further of her youth and innocence. No wonder her mother was worried — she appeared captivated by the duke.

"Good evening, Arden."

"Ockley," Arden greeted him. "I had thought you would be present tonight."

Leander bowed to Sophia. "Miss Westcourt, delighted."

She smiled warmly at him, a becoming colour staining her cheeks. "Lord Ockley," she welcomed, her eyes conveying her delight at seeing him.

"May I request the pleasure of your hand later?" he asked.

"A little forward in public, don't you think, Ockley?" Arden murmured very quietly.

Leander ignored him and engaged himself to a quadrille later in the evening. "I believe Lady Annesley is anxious to introduce you to an old friend who has just arrived," he concluded.

Miss Westcourt, with apparent reluctance, obeyed his unspoken injunction. Her mama immediately shepherded her to the other side of the room.

"I thought St George's reward was the fair maiden, not the dragon," Arden said, as Leander remained with him.

"I rather think we are supposed to believe that, as a Knight of the Church, he was chaste and so declined his prize," Leander said wryly.

"Poor St. George," Arden mused. "Still, I suppose virtue brings its own reward. Damned if I can see it though."

Leander laughed. "Are you not damned anyway?"

"True enough," Arden said. "Speaking of which, I was thinking of trying my luck at a new hell off Pall Mall tonight. Care to join me?"

Leander hesitated, torn.

Arden leaned in close to Leander so none would overhear him, his breath caressing his cheek. "Then you'll just have to dream of your reward, Leander. Have a virtuous evening."

With that, he turned and made his way from the crowded room, people moving to allow him unimpeded egress. Leander stared after him, damning his conscience, his mother, and his brother for not being there to take over responsibility for her. Most of all, he wondered at Arden's use of his first name, which suggested an intimacy between them.

After a moment he recollected himself, bit back his disappointment, and moved towards his partner for the next dance. Before he reached her, Lady Annesley descended upon him, declaring herself forever in his debt for rescuing her poor dear lamb from that man and for then routing him. "Dear Lord Ockley, I don't care what the rest of the world thinks—your brother's heroism doesn't hold a candle to you in *my* estimation."

"Thank you," Leander murmured dryly, freeing his sadly crushed sleeve from her eager grasp with a little difficulty before continuing towards his object.

Somehow he survived the evening, which rapidly descended into a particular form of torture, becoming a whirl of objectionable people claiming his notice, young ladies employing the arts of the coquette as they attempted to capture his obviously wandering attention, and capped off by a dance with Sophia that ended with that young lady almost in tears at Leander's heartless abstraction. She seemed crushed with disappointment after the warmth he had displayed earlier, and that led her into unbecoming frankness. She informed him that she wore Lord Ramsbottom's flowers, again. He nodded. She told him that Lord Ramsbottom had intimated he wished to make her an offer. He wished her happy. She asked him in a voice that trembled if he did not care for her. He asked her to repeat what she had said, for he had not quite heard it.

She did nothing that might invite censure, but the instant the dance ended, she left him standing and retreated to her mama's side. Leander had been surprised by the abruptness of her leaving and so he watched her to be sure all was well, noticing they left the ball shortly thereafter.

Determining that she must have the headache, he decided that he too should be allowed to plead exhaustion and retreat. His mama reluctantly allowed herself to be persuaded from Sir John Gillingham's flattering attentions and to be driven home.

Once his mother had retired, Leander found himself in the drawing room at Green Street, one arm leaning on the overmantel, a foot resting on the polished brass fireguard as he stared into the empty grate. He wondered if he might find his way to the new hell of which Arden had spoken. He angrily conceded that he did not know enough to find it. With that option denied him, he was not in the mood to find other company tonight. He wanted Caroline with an intensity that took him by surprise. Her continued absence had brought him to a new level of frustration. He could always find a lightskirt to release his desires, but Leander had seen the results of the pox. So he took himself to bed.

As soon as his valet left, Leander's hand went to his cock. He thought back to that scene in Arden's drawing room as his hand moved slowly, needing release but wanting to prolong the pleasure as long as possible. He wondered how it would feel to have a lady kneel in front of him so that he might thrust into her mouth, the way he had seen at Arden's house. As he thought back to that night, he remembered the sounds from Hazell and Farraday. Without volition, he found himself remembering the way Farraday had writhed so eagerly on Hazell's fingers.

Leander moved his hand faster, feeling the wetness on the head of his cock. Eyes closed, teeth biting into his lip to keep quiet, he thought of the woman on her knees, taking his cock, taking all of it into her warm mouth as Farraday's moans grew louder, and then Arden's voice in his ear asked him what he thought. Leander cried out as he came, his eyes tightly closed, desperately trying to summon a vision of Caroline to him. He failed.

CHAPTER NINE

The busy streets of London gave way to open country. Leander, his attention no longer on threading his match bays through traffic-filled thoroughfares, found his mind drifting back to his departure from Green Street. He had needed to employ firm measures with his mother to prevent an embarrassing scene.

He had sought her out in the drawing room to say his farewells, only to find her labouring under a strong sense of righteous indignation. She could not understand, indeed she *refused* to see, any possible reason for Leander to leave town at the height of the Season. As for her feelings upon learning — from *another*, moreover, not from her eldest son — that he would be a guest of that *dreadful* man . . .

Leander had eyed her narrowly. "My brother, I take it."

"There is no call to decry your brother for his sense of duty towards his mama." Her bosom swelled indignantly. "Precisely *when* did you intend to inform me of your destination, Leander? Do you have no consideration for the blow to my sensibilities it has been to find that you *know* that man? That you willingly will spend time as his *guest*?" Her eyes beseeched his tragically. "Have you *no* proper feeling?"

Emotion overcame her and she opened the vinaigrette she was clutching. Caught between annoyance and concern, Leander hesitated. At that moment, Henry entered the room. He checked on becoming aware of the atmosphere, before advancing to seat himself with every appearance of satisfaction.

"Tell him, Henry," the dowager appealed, with a pitiful

flutter of her hand towards her younger son. "Tell him he must not do such a thing."

Henry eyed his brother with disenchantment. "I expect that Lea will do whatever he wishes, regardless of your need for his support at this particular time, Mama."

The dowager looked as bewildered as Leander felt at these words.

"This particular time?" she asked

"The anniversary of dearest Papa's demise."

"Oh! Why, yes, to be sure, it is a *most* difficult time for me, and I would have hoped that you would remember that, Leander." The dowager opened her vinaigrette again, signalling just how emotionally difficult she found this time.

Leander forced himself to smile at her. "You have Henry's companionship, Mama. I know he will take the greatest care of you and bear you company wherever you wish."

Henry's brow was lowering. Before he could say anything, the dowager launched into another lament.

"If you *insist* on going, Leander, whatever shall I tell people? I *refuse* to repeat that you will be that man's guest. What in heaven's name possessed you to accept his invitation? You must know his shocking reputation. What will people *think*?"

Leander had finally been pushed into declaring that, as the head of the household, what he did was no one's business save his own. He was leaving now and would return to his house—a very slight emphasis on the possessive—when he chose, and only then. He bade them farewell and left.

By the time Leander reached his destination, many hours later, his unpleasant leave-taking was almost forgotten. As he swung his curricle neatly between two Cotswold stone pillars and past a substantial gatehouse, a sense of release and freedom ran through him.

Driving up the lengthy avenue, he looked with interest for

his first sight of Arden's country seat. Arden had told him that the original house, which the first duke had built, had been razed almost to the ground as the result of an unfortunate incident involving the third duke, a chicken, and a cigar. By way of expiation, the third duke – who had escaped from the blaze only slightly singed, which was more than could be said for the unlucky chicken – had built the magnificent edifice that now greeted Leander. The enormous house was a striking combination of classical Italian and Gothic, rendered in the same mellow Cotswold stone as the gatehouse. A fountain sparkled in the centre of the sweeping drive, but Leander scarcely noticed it, for the skyline of the house was the most extraordinary thing he had ever seen – a mass of pinnacles, chimneys, and turrets, and no evident order to be perceived.

As he drew the horses to a halt, a groom came to their heads. A swift glance to ensure the man knew how to treat his horses satisfied him, and he trod up the steps to the doors. What greeted him inside was as impressive as the exterior – a double-height entrance hall with fan-vaulted ceiling, and columns carrying a balustraded balcony.

Surrendering his many-caped driving coat, gloves, and hat into the keeping of a footman, Leander required the butler to take him to the other guests. He was impatient suddenly for congenial company. He knew they would forgive the travel-worn nature of his garments and that there was still time to change for dinner even if Arden kept country hours here.

He entered the Blue Drawing Room somewhat diffidently as he saw faces he recognised but no one he knew, and then he relaxed and smiled as Arden's unmistakable figure crossed the room towards him. Abruptly giddy with relief at the removal of any duty except to enjoy himself, Leander accepted the glass of sherry Arden pressed upon him and joined enthusiastically in the debate raging over the talents of some of the leading actresses.

By the time he came to change for dinner, Leander had im-
bibed generously enough to allow his valet unaccustomed liberties. When Morris finally allowed Leander out of his
clutches, Leander encountered Arden in the gallery outside
his bedchamber.

Arden's eyebrows raised. "Such splendour in my honour,
Leander. I'm overwhelmed."

Self-conscious, Leander glanced down at himself. His dark
green coat was unexceptionable, as were the pantaloons he
wore, but with repugnance he saw that Morris had triumphantly finished his outfit with multiple fobs, and a quizzing
glass hung on a riband around his neck. "God, I look like a
damned dandy," he said with loathing.

Arden laughed, then moved forward. "Let me assist you."
He concentrated on unfastening the fobs at Leander's waist.
Leander watched the dark head bent before him, breathing in
a strangely heady scent as he did so. By the time Arden looked
up, with the offending objects in his hand, Leander's face was
warm and the pace of his heart had quickened.

Arden's lips curved in a slow smile. "I should turn the fellow off, if I were you," he said. "He's evidently dressed you
too warmly."

It was true. Leander's clothes seemed to be clinging tightly
to him and perspiration was beginning to gather beneath his
shirt. A drop of sweat slid slowly down his spine as Arden
looked at him.

"Perhaps I should," he agreed automatically, uncomfortably aware that the sherry he had drunk appeared to have
robbed him of the ability to hold a sensible conversation. He
stood staring back into Arden's face until they were interrupted by Farraday's eruption from his bedchamber.

"Damnation, Arden," he demanded indignantly. "What
the devil do you mean by giving me a room full of paintings
of some damned female type wringing her hands and crying

over her dead child?"

Arden's eyes glinted with amusement as he turned to the indignant peer. "Come now, Farraday, that's one of my esteemed ancestors you're objecting to."

"Well, I'm sorry for you, Arden, that's all I can say." Farraday shuddered artistically. "Can't you do something about it?"

Arden sighed. "I'm sure I can have the painting removed if you find yourself unable to support its presence."

"I don't care what the devil you do with it, as long as you get rid of that damned depressing woman!"

Farraday's manner reminded Leander irresistibly of Henry. Arden's gaze let Leander know that he shared his amusement even while he assured Farraday that the offending picture would be removed before he had to brave his chamber again.

Proceeding downstairs, they found most of the party already gathered in the Green Drawing Room. Some were engaged in conversation over drinks, while several were arrayed at the long windows overlooking the drive. Intrigued, Leander joined them, wishing to see what held them so rapt.

The excited ladies descending from post chaises that had drawn up outside were—well, Leander supposed that they were best described as high fliers, dressed in finery the likes of which would not be seen at any respectable gathering. Except, that was, for the final lady. Her dress looked to be an exact copy of one that Leander had seen Lady Jersey wear to the opera—blue satin embroidered with white lilies and ornamented with pearl beads. It boasted a lace demi-train that the lady had caught up in one hand as she negotiated the steps of the chaise. A rather large hand, Leander could not help but notice, matching the angular arm that emerged from her sleeve. He looked from the lady to those around her, noting how tall she was and that her face was more heavily made up than any of her companions. Suspicion had already slid into his mind before he saw the lump beneath the velvet choker and that, at the low neck of the dress, no breasts swelled. The molly looked in the direction of the windows and, raising a hand to rouged lips, mimed a kiss at the watching gentlemen.

Farquhar turned to speak to the gentleman next to him and saw the shock on Leander's face. "Mistress Vestal," he said meaningfully.

Leander was suddenly adrift. He did not belong in company such as this, where outrageousness was not merely the aspiration but the norm. For the first time since meeting the man, he recollected the tales of the Duke of Arden's orgies. He had given them no credence, assuming the tales to be grossly overblown so that the worthy of the *ton* might condemn Arden's character with relish. He now realised how naïve he had been. He could not leave immediately — the afternoon was far advanced and the horses would not yet be recovered — but he did not wish to be party to such disgraceful things.

He turned from the window, all his pleasure in the day lost. Arden was beside him, pressing a glass into his hand. "I like to cater for the enjoyment of all my guests," he said. "They will be staying in the east wing and need not concern you, unless you wish it."

Leander emphatically did not wish it. Such arrangements in private were one thing, but this public flaunting went far beyond any concept of decency.

When the party proceeded to the dining room, Leander was deeply relieved to find only gentlemen filling the seats at the long table beneath the painted ceiling. As the meal progressed and Arden engaged him in conversation, he slowly forgot his unease. By the end of the evening, when he had not seen so much as the whisk of a petticoat, he could no longer remember why he had thought it so scandalous.

Leander was deep in his cups when he returned to his bed-chamber. A thump from next door announced Farraday's arrival just as Leander blew out his candle. He deduced that the painting Farraday had found so intolerable must have been removed. Either that, or he was no longer in a fit condition to notice. Smiling as he thought of the evening he had spent, the conversation he had enjoyed with Arden, and Arden's flattering attention, Leander slipped into a sound sleep.

He jerked awake and lay there, wondering what had woken him. He heard it again. A muffled moan. His brows drawing together, Leander sat up, wondering where it was coming from. There it was again. And then a gasping pleading, "Yes, now!"

His cheeks grew hot as he realised the cause of the noises from the room adjoining his. Sliding back beneath the covers, he punched the pillow into shape with enough force to drown out the sounds. Only temporarily, however. A low constant groaning became audible, punctuated with another man's grunts, then Farraday's unmistakable voice, pleading to be taken harder and faster, to be fucked until he couldn't stand. Leander pulled the pillow over his head. To no avail. The bed next door creaked rhythmically, the groans continued, and to his horror, Leander found himself becoming aroused by the sounds of pleasure.

He tried desperately to ignore his body's response, but as the sounds became wilder, as the grunts turned into gasping cries, he was powerless to stop himself from shaking free of the muffling pillow or to prevent his hand drifting to his cock. He groaned as his hand closed around the hot flesh. He began to work it in time with the cries from next door, trying to keep silent as his other hand trailed across his lips and his tongue flicked out to wet a finger. His throat dry, he swallowed hard as he drew that finger very lightly down his throat, across his collarbone, tracing an undeniable path to his nipple. The already tight flesh contracted further at his touch. Closing his eyes, he took the nipple between his fingers and rolled it as his other hand moved faster, finally pinching his nipple hard as his hand tightened convulsively around his cock. His cry as his warm seed spilled over his skin was drowned by the abandoned sounds of ecstasy from next door.

Leander lay in the dark, panting. The noises from the next room changed to the low murmur of conversation, a characteristic laugh informing Leander that Farraday's visitor was none other than Sir Richard Hazell. An inexplicable wave of melancholy hit Leander as he imagined them lying there, holding one another. He turned over in his bed and willed sleep to return. Eventually, it did.

Leander drifted slowly awake, taking a moment to remember where he was. Daylight from between imperfectly drawn drapes lightened the room, but the sound of rain lashing against the window panes persuaded him to stay in his warm bed a while longer. His valet had not yet appeared, although that gave Leander little clue as to the time. He had informed Morris that he would not be needed before midday for the duration of their stay. In doing so, he'd followed the advice of the other gentlemen, all of whom had previously attended Arden's house parties. They had indicated it was most unlikely any of the guests would arise until the afternoon due to the hours kept by the duke.

He stretched, luxuriating in the sensation of waking muscles and wondering what the day had in store. Last night he had eagerly accepted Arden's invitation to ride out with him, but there would be little pleasure even in Arden's company in hacking in this weather. Out of season, there was no hunting and little shooting to tempt any of the party outside and no other reason for them to venture out in such persistent rain.

The previous night, some of the company had engaged in rounds of Hazard. Others, like he and Arden, had played billiards. Yet others had passed their evening in the company of the ladybirds, evidently knowing just which drawing rooms they should visit to do so.

Perhaps today would be a repeat of those entertainments, only a little less well-lubricated. However the day was spent, Leander reflected, it would bear no comparison to the tedium and claustrophobia of *tonnish* life. He spared a brief thought for his mother and Henry, wondering idly which of them he felt most sorry for, having been left with the other. A sound from next door took the smile from his face.

He glanced at the wall between the two rooms, unwillingly reminded of the activity that had disturbed his sleep and wondering how noise could travel so clearly through solid stone. In the daylight, his question was answered. A door in the wall connected the two rooms. Although solidly built, the door was ill-fitting, and sounds from next door were audible in Leander's silent chamber. Unmistakable sounds that would not stop and could not be ignored. The sound of a hand meeting softer flesh in a series of hard slaps. Each slap was followed immediately by a gasp, a plea, a begging, "Harder, please Richard, harder." But the slaps kept their slow rhythm, causing Farraday to beg more loudly, more desperately. Then there was silence. Leander strained his ears to find out why.

His mouth opened in shock as the silence was broken by the brutal smack of leather against skin. There was a cry of pain, then one of outrage. "Don't stop, for God's sake Richard, do it. Please." Again, leather meeting flesh, the cry, followed by a groan. "More, God, more." Quicker now, groans almost constant, the slap of leather punctuated by Hazell's growled commands.

Leander lay rigid in his bed, trying to deny what he was

hearing and encouraging the sense of revulsion he knew he should be feeling. The sounds continued unabated.

In desperation, he rose from his bed and strode across the room to the pitcher and bowl on the dresser. Pouring water into the bowl, he reached for the cloth and sponged himself. Farraday was whimpering now — pain or pleasure, Leander couldn't tell, as the leather continued its inexorable assault.

Looking down, Leander saw the cloth in his hand slowly circling his left nipple, again and again, long after it was necessary. He abruptly threw the cloth into the bowl and snatched up a towel. Drying himself roughly, he looked around for a shirt. What in hell had his damned man done with them? He finally located one and pulled it on over his head with clumsy hands, only realising his mistake as the fine lawn slipped down his body, trailing over his skin with a soft caress.

He gave up the unequal fight. Drawing the ends of the shirt aside, Leander wrapped a comforting hand around himself. Nothing more than that, certainly not to stroke his straining flesh in time with the groans from next door, the sound of leather on flesh, the wild urging for Hazell to continue, harder, to make him come. Leander's hand stilled as, with a string of wild sounds, Farraday reached his completion.

Leander stood, head down, eyes closed, breathing fast, torn between relief and overwhelming disappointment. He could finish himself in an efficient manner without being troubled by the inappropriate sounds from next door. He felt disappointed because he would now have to be silent, that was all.

As he began to move his hand again, a raw voice sounded through the door. "Suck me."

Screwing his eyelids together more tightly, Leander tried not to think of the scene playing out only yards from him. Of Farraday, perhaps spattered with his seed, sore and bruised, kneeling before Hazell. Of Hazell wrapping his hands in

Farraday's hair, driving into the welcoming mouth, fucking it hard until he was groaning. Leander's thrusts into his hand were in time, soft moans escaping him as Hazell groaned, and then as the pace quickened, both thrust faster, deeper, feeling it build, needing release, desperate to come, desperate . . . oh, *God*. Leander's knees buckled. He made a wild grab at the side of the bed as the world tipped around him.

He opened his eyes to find himself on his knees and the counterpane pulled half off the bed. He buried his face in the covers where he was clutching them, aware of the lonely scent of his seed. He knelt there in the silence, waiting for his heart rate to slow, for his breathing to steady. Waiting for . . . something.

CHAPTER TEN

The rain continued with the enthusiasm it reserved solely for an English spring day, and the party separated into smaller groups to pursue their own pleasures in such inclement weather. Leander found Arden at his side, offering to show him round the house. He accepted the invitation with alacrity and spent a pleasant time listening to Arden's biting commentary on architectural and furnishing choices made by certain of his ancestors. As they proceeded through the west wing, Leander was pleased to find Arden's promise about the ladybird visitors held true and that he saw no trace of them. Indeed, there were scarcely signs of any of the party in the massive house, which possessed more staircases, passageways, and rooms than Leander could begin to catalogue.

When they reached the Long Gallery, which ran the entire width of the house, Leander was drawn to the portraits on the walls. He was curious to see Arden's forebears. The paintings were of the third duke onwards, earlier ones having been lost when the original house had burned. There was a strong family resemblance in the male line of the family. Leander found his gaze flicking between the paintings and the man at his side to verify this. The same dark eyes and hair, the same full lips. Even the faintly ridiculous fashions of yesteryear could not hide the muscular build common to many of the Ravensburg family through the years.

The portraits ended with Arden's father, to whose likeness Leander paid particular attention. Although the faces were alike, he could see nothing of Arden in the man. True, he had a similarly haughty head carriage, but there was none of the mockery with which the present duke surveyed the world.

"There is no portrait of you?" he asked.

Arden's laughter held an unpleasant tone. "Do you think I wish to sit for hours before some damned artist, simply to satisfy the vanity of a family of which I am the only surviving member?"

The question seemed rhetorical, so Leander made no answer. He studied instead a painting of a lady with soft brown hair, and a spaniel at her feet. "Your mother?" Leander ventured, for the portrait hung close to that of the previous duke.

"My grandmother," Arden said, his voice clipped.

Leander was puzzled. The painting was the final female portrait in the series, which meant there was no portrait of his mother. Arden's manner warned him not to persist with his questions, so he moved along the gallery to the series of engravings that followed the portraits.

After an instant of shock, his cheeks heated. They were engravings the likes of which he had not previously encountered. Their artistic merit might be questionable, but that was not their purpose. He flicked a sideways glance at Arden, wondering at the man shamelessly displaying these alongside his family portraits. Arden was watching him, amusement in his face.

"An interesting collection," Leander managed. "Is the accumulation of such pieces your work or a family tradition?"

"I feel it incumbent upon me to patronise struggling artists." Arden looked over the pictures before him before adding, "I believe this one to show particular talent."

Leander obediently moved to look at the engraving Arden indicated, only to become further discomposed. The others had been of men and women, but the one before him was of a man thrusting into another man from behind, the artist capturing in exquisite detail the moment when all control was gone and both were lost in ecstasy.

"It has some merit," Leander agreed, his voice tight. Was that how Farraday and Hazell had looked last night?

"This is one of his also."

Leander withdrew his gaze from the picture before him and joined Arden, who was standing with folded arms, surveying an engraving with an expression of satisfaction. Leander wished above all for this to end. There were not many pictures left before the end of the gallery. Please God, may Arden not want him to examine every piece of priapic art between where they now stood and the doorway. He turned his attention to the one before him. The central figure was a naked man, his arms outstretched, chained between two pillars. Figures crouched at his feet, working their way up his thighs, tongues snaking over flesh, while he was taken from behind. Leander stared at the picture for a moment before he saw the figure watching from the back of the room, sprawled on his seat in a strangely familiar manner.

He looked away abruptly, unsettled in a way he did not understand. "He's good," he agreed again. He hardly knew what he said, his eyes falling on another engraving with yet more naked men in the throes of passionate copulation.

Before Arden could draw his attention to any more pieces, Leander made his way to the doorway at the end of the gallery. To his infinite relief, Arden didn't call him back. He descended a short staircase and ventured into a room that opened to the right-hand side, deeply thankful to find it harboured no exotic art or sculpture. The room was small, relative to the titanic proportions of the house, and held a few pieces of Jacobean furniture along with paintings of gamebirds and gundogs. Above the fireplace hung as deadly looking a pair of gold-mounted pistols as he had ever seen.

Swiftly crossing the room, Leander lifted one down, enjoying its weight and balance. It was a weapon meant for business, but there would also be pleasure in its employ. He sighted experimentally along the barrel at a painting on the opposite wall.

"It throws a trifle left," Arden said. "Permit me."

Standing behind Leander, his right arm followed the path of Leander's arm and his hand closed around Leander's wrist, moving it the appropriate amount to counter the action of the weapon. Leander stood very still. Arden's arm was against his, their bodies were close, and Arden's warm breath stirred his hair. When Arden stepped back, Leander found the room oddly cold. He held the gun a moment longer for form's sake before relinquishing it.

While Arden returned it to its original position on the wall, Leander paced jerkily to look out of the window. The rain was still relentless.

"Do you care to fence?"

He turned to see an almost feral smile on Arden's face.

"A capital idea," he agreed, excitement rippling through him at the thought of some activity on this day of unforeseen incarceration.

A footman brought Arden's foils at his command. They stripped off their coats and returned to the gallery, where Arden offered Leander his choice of foil.

The long stretch of oak floor allowed unimpeded movement, and Leander swiftly recognised he was outclassed. He had a quick eye and a supple wrist, but he was no natural at this. His preferred weapon was the pistol—he was well known at Manton's Gallery as a deadly accurate shot. Arden, on the other hand, fought with a pace and enjoyment that conveyed his love of the art. His swift moves were disconcertingly unpredictable to his opponent, his teeth bared in a smile as he employed them, but his intent gaze spoke of the careful planning underlying each. Though he might look to be an undisciplined fighter, every move and countermove was thought out.

Leander found himself hard-pressed, sweating as he was forced onto the defensive. Arden was steadily moving him back along the gallery, his lips drawn back in that same smile even though he was breathing more quickly now, his eyes alight with enjoyment and his body tireless. For an instant, Leander was fatally distracted by the lightness of Arden's moves, seeing the answer in the muscled thighs that absorbed the shock of his rapid foot movements. Arden took advantage of his inattention to break through his guard. Moving swiftly, Leander managed to deflect his lunge so the point of Arden's foil caught his right arm instead of coming to rest on his breast.

Aggrieved at himself for giving away the contest before it had reached its natural conclusion, Leander allowed his foil to drop until the end touched the floor. "The victory is yours," he admitted, breathing heavily.

Arden's foil clattered to the floor and he was at Leander's side. "My dear Leander, are you hurt? The button must have come off my foil. I would not have such an unfortunate incident happen for the world."

Leander stared nonplussed for an instant before following Arden's gaze to the right sleeve of his white shirt. He saw a fresh red stain, growing by the second. Lost in the excitement of the contest, Leander hadn't sensed when the point had caught him, but now that he saw the blood, he felt the sting of a wound.

"I'm perfectly well," he muttered, embarrassed.

"Let me see," Arden commanded peremptorily. When Leander made no instant move, he insisted. "For God's sake, man, take off your shirt. Let me see."

Leander laid his blade to one side and reluctantly ruined his careful work with his neckcloth before removing his waistcoat. Unfastening his shirt, he slipped it over his head and found that the injury appeared to be a clean one.

Nevertheless, Arden directed him to be seated on one of the chairs placed against the wall. Taking up the discarded neck-cloth, he knelt beside Leander and firmly pressed the folded cloth to the injury to arrest any further bleeding.

Leander sat in his breeches, light-headed as Arden's breath moved against his bare skin. The blood loss was responsible, he realised, but it was not an unpleasant feeling. As though dreaming, he slowly became aware that Arden had removed the makeshift pad and he felt another sensation. He looked down at his arm to see Arden's tongue moving over the site of his wound. Startled, he pulled away with an oath.

Arden raised mocking eyes to his. "My apologies, Leander, for taking you by surprise, but human saliva holds healing qualities," he explained. "It cleanses the wound — any leech worth his salt will tell you that."

A trifle self-conscious, Leander moved back to his previous position. "You surprised me," he said in apology.

Arden looked at him, eyes gleaming. "Yes, I can see I did." His head lowered to Leander's upper arm before he looked up at Leander again. "You don't object, do you?"

"I don't." As he felt the warm tongue against his flesh, that was the truth. Licking him, cleaning the oozing blood from the wound with slow, deliberate sweeps, seeming to draw patterns on his flesh. Leander was floating, unwilling to come back to reality. The injury stung, but that soft tongue wiped the pain away.

He drifted, eyes closing as Arden's mouth worked its magic. Only slowly did he become aware of the increasing constriction of his breeches, announcing his cock's reaction to the pleasurable sensation. In concert with that response, Leander was aware that his nipples were beginning to tighten. He had not seen Caroline for too long, that was the trouble. His body was ready to treat any touch from another as stimulation. He sat as still as he could, hoping desperately that

Arden had not noticed his inappropriate reaction to a simple piece of medical attention.

"I believe the patient will survive."

Leander's eyes opened at the familiar mocking tone to find Arden standing and extending a hand to help him to his feet.

Arden accompanied him to his chamber so he could change his ruined shirt and neckcloth, staying close beside him the entire way lest he become faint. It was with a sense of loss that Leander stood at the door of his room and watched him walk away.

Leander was still a trifle light-headed when he joined the party before dinner. A swift glance around the assembled company informed him that Arden was not yet present, so he joined the group closest to him, consisting of Farraday, Sir Rupert Ogborne, and Edmund Roslyn. Each time he looked at Farraday, he found himself reminded of the sounds from the previous night, accompanied by visions of the engravings.

Lost in involuntary reflections, Leander was surprised when the company began to move into the dining room. He hadn't noticed Arden's arrival. When his group reached the table, he was disappointed to find the seats beside Arden already filled. He had discovered the previous evening that no formalities such as seating by rank were in force here.

With a conscious effort, Leander took a more active part in the conversation around him. He had, after all, enjoyed Arden's company for most of the day, as well as the previous evening. It was unreasonable of him to expect any more. The gentlemen around him were pleasant enough company, Leander supposed. He had to suppress a grin as he compared this to what he would have been subjected to were he still in London. They were wonderful company, he amended, and he joined in their light-hearted banter with renewed vigour.

As had been the case the previous night, the wine flowed

freely and the party grew louder and less inhibited as the meal progressed. Leander's enjoyment was dimmed slightly by the fact that, each time he looked, Arden appeared to be deep in conversation with Asbury, seated beside him. He thrust that away and allowed himself to be entertained by Broughton's seemingly endless fund of scandalous stories about Wellington, one of whose staff officers happened to be Broughton's younger brother. Committing some of these tales to memory, he anticipated repeating them to Henry and Burnage. They would, Leander was sure, relish them as much as did the assembled company.

After the servants were dismissed, when port was being drunk and snuff taken, Leander was brought to a realisation that shocked him from his haze of well-being. As he reached yet again for his glass, a laugh breaking from him at the latest outrageous claim from Broughton, a movement to his left caught his attention. A glance was sufficient to inform him that Roslyn's hand was on Farraday's thigh. Not merely resting there as he made a conversational point but stroking it. Farraday's legs parted, and Roslyn moved his hand towards where Farraday's cock was increasingly evident, swelling against his pantaloons.

Leander jerked his gaze away. He had thought that Hazell was Farraday's lover, but Hazell was seated further along the table. He was either unconcerned or unaware of what was taking place. As Leander looked more closely, he could not be sure that a similar scenario was not taking place between Hazell and his neighbour.

Disconcerted, Leander took a deep draught from his glass. He was not surprised, precisely. He knew of Farraday's and Hazell's proclivities and had not forgotten their previous public uninhibited expression of these. But to indulge these with partners other than each other, and to do so at the dining table, moreover when seated close beside him, disturbed him greatly.

In his determination to look anywhere but at what was taking place next to him, Leander's gaze found Ogborne's blond good looks across the table. Ogborne met his eyes with a suggestive smile. He dipped a finger in his port, lifted it to his lips and slowly sucked the liquid from it, holding Leander's gaze the entire time. Leander thrust his chair back with a muttered excuse and left the room.

Finding sanctuary in a nearby parlour, he rested his forehead against the window. As he stared into the grey evening outside, the part of his mind that was attempting to distract him from recent events noted that it had, at last, stopped raining. His cheeks heated anew as he realised what he had done, rushing from the table like some schoolroom miss. He was not a stranger to the habits of Arden's friends, after all. It had been the proximity to him of what had been going on that had so disturbed him. That, and the unmistakable invitation from Ogborne. Leander was prepared to ignore the inclinations of those around him in order to enjoy Arden's company, but to find that he was now considered to be a possible player in their games . . . He breathed deeply, trying to calm the sudden quivering inside him at the thought.

Eventually, he turned from the window, wondering what he should do. He preferred not to run the gauntlet of returning to the dining room. In any case, he suspected that Farraday and Roslyn would still be indulging themselves and he did not wish to be seated beside them whilst they did so. No, the company would soon break up into smaller groups as they had done the previous evening. When that had happened, Arden had retired to the billiard room with Leander and a few others.

Leander found his way to the room in question. Oil lamps were already lit, indicating an expectation it would be used. He settled himself in a chair and waited, glad of the room's proximity to the dining room so that he might hear when the party finally adjourned.

It was a full twenty minutes later, according to the ormolu clock on the mantelshelf, when a brief increase in noise announced that the dining room door had opened and closed. Leander waited hopefully, but whoever had left had taken themselves elsewhere. He sat there, watching the filigree hands of the clock move with agonising slowness. Occasional bursts of uproarious laughter came from the dining room, but there was no sign of the party moving elsewhere. He remained undisturbed even by servants in his solitude and the room grew slowly darker as twilight fell.

Growing ever more uncomfortable, Leander finally went looking for company. He knew there was at least one other no longer at the table. He made his way along the west corridor of the house, opening doors at random, hoping for company or, at the very least, some sort of diversion. He stood in the doorway to the Yellow Parlour for an instant too long before stepping sharply backwards.

Blindly he sought the door to the gardens and escaped into the damp evening air, desperate to find sanctuary. He made it to the shelter of the line of elm trees and leaned against the wide trunk of one of these for support, lifting his hot face to the skies in denial. Yet all he could see was the tableau that had greeted him in the Yellow Parlour—Hazell on his knees in front of Arden, unbuttoning his pantaloons. Leander wrenched at his damnably tight neckcloth as he denied the moment when Arden had looked up and seen Leander standing there, watching in shock, and had smiled. Oh, *God*.

Stumbling slightly as he moved, Leander ran. Over the soaking grass, along the path, gravel spurting beneath his feet. Away from the house, away from the sight of Arden with Hazell, away from the laughter and the wine and the confusion.

CHAPTER ELEVEN

He came to a panting halt where the lawn beside the lake gave way to shrubs. Ripping off his constricting neckcloth, he tried to restore some sort of order to his thoughts. What did it signify if he had borne unwilling witness to disconcerting sights this evening? He knew Arden's reputation. Had he really expected the man to be a monk?

He swallowed convulsively, still breathing hard, though he no longer thought it from exertion, and railed at himself for his extraordinary reaction. And then he stopped breathing altogether. There was a familiar presence behind him and that well-known mocking voice.

"A little damp for a stroll, don't you think, Leander?"

Leander tried desperately to return his breathing pattern to normal. He wouldn't—*couldn't*—turn and face Arden. Not yet. Not until he could look at him without seeing the intent expression on his face as he had watched Hazell unfastening his pantaloons. Leander remained facing the lake in the dusk, unable to speak.

Arden moved close behind him. Leander concentrated on breathing. The warmth of Arden's body close to his, the heat of his breath on Leander's neck, the caress of Arden's voice in his ear. "Leander . . ."

"What?" His voice was a breathless croak.

"I think—no, I am certain—it is going to rain again. Which leads me to wonder why you decided to take a walk in such weather."

Leander swallowed and swivelled on his heel to face

Arden. "It was warm," he managed. "Too much wine." His eyes met Arden's dark gaze and his mouth dried. His heart beat faster.

"Why did you leave, Leander?" Arden's smooth voice made him shiver.

Why had he left? What had there been to shock him, to overset him so in what he had seen? It was nothing he did not know to be true about Arden. His breath came fast and he couldn't tear his eyes from Arden's. The duke was only inches from him, close enough for Leander to feel his hot breath against his cheek. He imagined he felt the warmth emanating from that powerful body even through the shirt and waistcoat, the tight pantaloons that he had just seen unfastened . . .

"I want you." Leander's words seemed to hang in the evening air. He stared at Arden, unwilling to believe that they had come from his mouth.

Arden moved until they were touching. The length of his body pressed against Leander's, leaving Leander breathless in disbelief as Arden's lips moved closer to his. His mouth opened — to say no, to tell him this was a mistake, this wasn't what he had meant, this wasn't what he wanted. But then full lips were on his and a tongue slid into his mouth. Leander whimpered as Arden's tongue stroked against his. Arden slid his arms around Leander, bringing their bodies still closer as he did so. Leander froze in shock as he felt an unmistakable hardness pressing against him through the material of their pantaloons. His eyes closed in denial as his cock filled in response.

He felt Arden's hands removing his waistcoat and then he was allowing his shirt to be pulled over his head. He was shivering in the evening air, waiting for the touch he knew would follow. He knew this had to stop, but his nipples were tight, aching with need. The dizzying warmth moved from his mouth and a warm tongue swiped across one nipple. He cried out and opened his eyes, looking down to see the dark head bent to his chest while Arden's hands worked on the fall of his pantaloons. Leander's cock jerked at the realisation and he whimpered again, even while he knew he had to stop this before it went any further. Before it went too far.

Then his cock was freed and Arden was on his knees before Leander. He watched in dry-mouthed disbelief as Arden reached for him, his fingers moving across the smooth head of his cock before his hand wrapped around the hard flesh and guided it towards his mouth. Leander's head fell back and he groaned helplessly as Arden swallowed him. The only thing keeping Leander upright was the pressure of Arden's hands on his thighs, refusing to let his knees buckle under the unbelievable sensations as Arden's tongue moved against him. He started jerkily to push into Arden's mouth, closing his mind to what he was doing, aware only of his cock.

Just as he registered that the warmth around him had gone, Arden's hands wrapped behind his knees, gently pulling Leander down to kneel opposite him in the wet grass. This time it was he who reached towards Arden, and his was the tongue that pushed into the other's mouth.

They were pressed tightly together, the buttons of Arden's waistcoat hard against his chest, and then Arden was moving him backwards till he lay on the soaking grass. His revulsion at the cold wetness was lost when Arden kissed him once more and touched his body, exploring with his hands in a way that left Leander writhing, incoherent with pleasure.

Arden pulled back after a while and moved further down Leander's body, removing his pantaloons. Leander lay still, dazed, as they were pulled off. By the time Arden returned to kneel astride Leander's body, Leander's breathing was fast and uncontrolled. He stared up at Arden's face in the gloom, then his eyes lowered to where Arden's cock was thrusting against his pantaloons. Swallowing slightly, he reached out an uncertain hand and touched it. Arden's sound of pleasure encouraged him, and he stroked it, aware that Arden's eyes were steady on his face. Emboldened, Leander unfastened Arden's fall, staring at what was thus revealed. Arden's cock was big, dark and hard, the head wet. Leander reached out to touch the shaft, encouraged again by the noise Arden made. Then Arden was moving further up his body and offering his cock to Leander's mouth.

Leander hesitated. He had never — He didn't know how — He shouldn't — But the tip was inches from his lips, the scent of Arden filling his senses. Leander's tongue flicked out and he caught the drop of liquid on the smooth head. The salty taste barely had time to register before Arden was feeding his cock into Leander's suddenly willing mouth. He relaxed his muscles to allow the length in as far as it could go, and then he didn't know what to do. His dilemma was solved as Arden pulled almost completely out before pushing himself back into Leander's mouth. Leander caught at the cock with his lips as it came back in, determined not to let it go again, sucking desperately to keep the cock there, to keep Arden inside him. A gasp, then a low laugh from Arden as he pulled back slightly before sliding in again between willing lips.

"You like it, Leander, don't you?" he asked, his voice deep. He thrust faster, making a noise of satisfaction each time he slid home. Leander sucked harder, breathless sounds escaping him around the hard flesh.

Suddenly Arden was pulling away from him, leaving him. Leander's chagrined eyes sought Arden's face. He hadn't done it properly. He hadn't been good enough for Arden. His fears eased as he watched Arden stand up and strip himself of his neckcloth, waistcoat, and shirt, his gaze on Leander's face as he did so. He set the toe of one shoe behind the heel of the other and rid himself of it in a way that would strike horror into the heart of any self-respecting valet. A similar move and the other shoe was gone before Arden peeled off his pantaloons and stockings and stood naked in the twilight.

Leander looked up at his beautiful body and shivered at the knowledge he was complicit in his own corruption. More than that—willing. Part of his brain had refused to stop screaming its outrage at what was happening. Leander had tried to believe it was the wine that caused his behaviour and that Arden had continued despite Leander's desire for him to stop. The act of waiting for Arden gave the lie to it all. Whatever the consequences might be, he was desperate to feel Arden's touch once more. The Earl of Ockley lay on his back in the gathering dusk and waited.

Arden's gaze was drawn to his cock. Leander's pulse was racing, his heart pounding as Arden again knelt on the grass, this time between his legs, pushing them apart before he moved his hands to Leander's thighs and held him down. Leander raised his head and watched, and then he was arching backwards, crying out incoherently as Arden licked his cock. Leander writhed in the merciless hold, desperate as Arden's tongue trailed up the sensitive skin. Eventually, Arden reached the head of his cock and his tongue swirled lightly across the tip, taking liquid, leaving his moisture in its place. Leander was sobbing with every breath he took by the time Arden finally stopped, only to turn his attention to Leander's balls, his hot tongue unrelenting.

"God, no." Leander was begging, tearing chunks out of the immaculate lawn beneath him with his hands as he thrashed on the wet grass, but Arden's unforgiving attentions continued.

Just when Leander knew he would die if it didn't stop, Arden raised his head to look at Leander, his breath coming faster. The smile on his lips as he looked found an immediate response in the jerk of Leander's thick cock. Arden looked down at it and extended a finger to catch the moisture at the tip before moving so that he was astride Leander. Leaning forward, he offered it to Leander. Leander snatched eagerly, greedily at the proffered finger, tasting himself on Arden, sucking the finger in, unwilling to let it go.

He stared up into Arden's dark eyes as his tongue wrapped again and again around the finger and he sucked desperately. Despite his efforts, Arden removed his finger and replaced it with his tongue. Leander moaned into Arden's mouth as that tongue probed his mouth, only for his eyes to close in unbelieving ecstasy as Arden's nails grazed his nipples and his cock moved against Leander's. He was thrusting upwards frantically, needing to rub his cock against Arden's, wanting to feel his hard flesh sliding against Arden's beautiful cock until they both came.

His eyes snapped open as Arden moved off him. Arden was bending to his waistcoat, removing a small bottle from the pocket. He returned to kneel between Leander's legs again and opened the bottle. Leander's head raised and he watched in sudden apprehension. This was really going to happen. He shivered suddenly. What in damnation did he think he was doing, lying naked on his back on soaking wet grass, with this notorious rake naked and erect between his open legs?

Before his mind could go any further along that path, Arden bent his head to Leander's abruptly softening cock. The delirious pleasure of that tongue gently tracing the slit while one hand caressed his balls sent Leander arching backwards on the grass, welcoming its slippery cold touch on his overheated skin, his cock hard again, thrusting his hips up in desperate invitation for Arden to continue.

As Arden's mouth continued its work on his cock, the hand that had been gently stroking his balls traced a path downwards. Leander groaned and spread his thighs further, encouraging that finger as it stroked his tender skin. Arden's full lips were closed around the very tip of Leander's cock, his tongue lightly flicking and teasing the sensitive head, denying all of Leander's despairing efforts to thrust further into his mouth. The tongue continued its delicious work, leaving Leander gasping and shuddering with need until, with no warning, Arden pushed his mouth down on Leander's cock.

When Arden released him and he could breathe again, Leander realised that Arden's finger was now inside him. His discomfort at the idea was lost as the probing finger brushed against a place that had him crying out, writhing wildly, desperate to feel that sensation again. By the time Arden had two fingers inside him, Leander was whimpering to the darkening sky, helpless to do anything save react to Arden's touch.

He cried out in distress when the fingers withdrew, raising his head to demand of Arden what the hell he thought he was doing. What he saw had him breathing raggedly. Arden was smoothing some of the liquid from the bottle over his hard cock, a lingering touch on his own flesh as he watched Leander. Leander reached out to feel the slickness of oil coating the hard flesh, loving the way Arden's eyes lidded slightly and he groaned softly at the touch. Then Leander's legs were being moved and the blunt head of Arden's cock was against him. Leander gasped as Arden's size began to fill him, stretching him. God, it hurt, but it felt like nothing he had ever known.

Arden pushed all the way inside him. Dimly remembering one of the engravings he had seen, Leander wrapped his legs around Arden's back to allow him even deeper. His reward was a groan from Arden at his movement and then deep thrusts. Leander was arching and writhing as the cock touched that place inside him, filling him, over and over again. His nails left trails of need across Arden's skin. "Oh, God."

Arden gasped out his pleasure as he voraciously watched his cock thrusting into Leander's arse, before his gaze was greedy on Leander's face. Leander was beyond sense, beyond anything except the feel of Arden's cock inside him as he pushed faster into Leander. Leander cried out wordlessly as he came, and Arden's hips lost their rhythm and he emptied himself deep inside Leander with a cry of savage triumph.

He slumped forward and they lay in the near-darkness, hearts racing, sweat mingling. Dazed, Leander held Arden to him. As their breathing steadied and he could feel Arden's heart rate slowing, Arden gave a low laugh and moved to lie beside him.

"You'd think in this damnable climate we might at least have had the sense to move indoors."

Leander's eyes were on his face, trying to read his expression in the fast-fading light. Not knowing what to think, Leander decided as a consequence to think nothing at all. He was distracted from the confusion in his head by the realisation that the moisture on his skin was no longer sweat, as he had thought, but the ominous beginnings of rain. Large cold drops splashed slowly but relentlessly.

"I rest my case," Arden concluded, climbing to his feet and picking up his clothes.

His mind carefully blank, Leander stood up and, following Arden's example, pulled his pantaloons on, fighting to drag the damp material over wet thighs. As the rain fell faster, he decided not even to attempt his shirt and they moved quickly through the rain back to the house, only just able to see their way in the falling darkness.

The house struck warm as they entered and Leander blinked in the sudden light. They encountered no one on their way upstairs, for which Leander was deeply thankful, given how they must look—half-naked with soaking hair, and pantaloons clinging wetly. The injury to his arm had begun to bleed again at some point, and Arden had some betraying marks on his body. Leander swallowed hard as he saw them in the light, trying to deny the incontrovertible reminders of his wild abandon

Upon reaching the landing, he turned left to go to his bed-chamber, only for Arden to call him back. "Where are you go-ing, Leander? Come and dry yourself."

Leander needed to be alone. He needed to understand what had happened, to work out how he could face Arden again. Yet the manners so carefully inculcated in him since childhood meant he did not like to refuse outright.

"Come, Leander," Arden invited again, turning and mak-ing his way towards his room.

Leander stood there until he heard voices and footsteps crossing the hall, sounding as if their owners were about to mount the stairs. Not wishing to be discovered in such a con-dition, he helplessly followed the way Arden had gone.

Standing in the doorway of Arden's dressing room, he found Arden towelling his hair before the roaring fire in the hearth. Arden glanced up, fixing him with his dark gaze.

Lost, Leander felt that he was trapped in some sort of dis-turbing dream. Soon he would awaken to normal life. He would dress and partake of breakfast in the parlour that his mother favoured for this meal, before retiring to his book room to read the newspaper. If this contained news of Henry's regiment being engaged against the foe — or, more alarmingly, reference to Henry's latest daring exploits, how-ever anonymised they might be — he would rehearse a reas-suring version. He would then seek out the dowager to break the news gently to her before one of her cronies thoughtlessly asked about it.

Later, he might go to Manton's Gallery, or perhaps he would visit Jackson's Saloon to engage in a bout of sparring. He would take a quiet luncheon, and, if he were particularly fortunate, there would be decisions concerning the estate that would require his attention, or possibly Caroline might be amenable to an afternoon visit. Later in the day, he would ride in the park, where it was not permitted to exceed a sedate canter. And then he would submit again to his valet and emerge ready to escort his mama to yet another interminable social gathering where no one said anything yet everyone spoke.

He kicked the door closed behind him. For better or for worse, and he truly didn't know which this was, he was making his choice. Regardless of the hint of surprise in Arden's eyes, Leander took the towel from his hands and rubbed it over Arden's chest, the coarse fibre stimulating cold wet skin, the friction against Arden's nipples bringing them to tight buds.

Leander leaned in and flicked one with his tongue, his eyes closing as he drowned in Arden's scent and taste. Arden's hand stroked Leander's arse, exploring the curves so clearly outlined by the clinging wet material, before his other hand wrapped in his hair and pulled his head back so that Leander was staring into the dark face above him. The familiar mocking smile was on Arden's lips, yet the customary gleam in his eye was anything but lazy as his mouth descended on Leander's.

CHAPTER TWELVE

Waking to the body next to his, Leander moved closer into the comforting warmth. Caroline and he did not often fall asleep together, and now, as always, it answered a need in him more profound than the physical. He breathed in deeply, prolonging the moment, knowing he would soon have to wake her and leave. He must not stay too long lest gossip start. Expecting to inhale Caroline's light fragrance, his eyes opened in shock at the unmistakably male dusky scent in his nostrils. It took a moment to register the unpalatable truth that his face was pressed against a muscular arm.

Pulling sharply backwards in consternation, Leander saw long dark hair spilling onto the white pillowcase. With a flooding of heat to his face, he remembered. He recalled writhing in wanton abandon on the wet grass, desperate for Arden to take him. The unaccustomed soreness in his body reminded him further.

He lay motionless, holding himself rigidly away from Arden. He had no idea how Arden would react to him this morning nor how he in turn should act. As though aware of his thoughts, Arden stretched slightly, then thrust down the covers and turned onto his side to face Leander. Leander swallowed at the broad expanse of chest that filled his vision before he dared to look at Arden's face.

"Good morning, Leander." Arden greeted him matter-of-factly, a glint in his eyes letting Leander know that he was fully aware of his uncertainty before full warm lips descended on his mouth. He knew a moment of shock, an instant of fear, and then his senses were swamped as Arden's tongue pushed into his mouth. Arden explored with an intensity that caused Leander to tangle his hands in Arden's hair, holding him so that he would never leave.

Arden pulled him closer, and as he felt the warmth and fullness moving against his morning erection, Leander moaned into his mouth. He moved his hands over Arden's body, stilling suddenly at the unfamiliar feeling of clearly defined muscles rather than slender limbs and soft skin. This was so different . . . Leander had sometimes felt that he overwhelmed Bella. He was so much bigger and stronger than she, and his need at times so great, that he had feared he would hurt her if he were to give in completely to his passion. Memories of Bella wavered and dissolved as he succumbed to the pleasure of the moment, his strong hands exploring Arden's body.

Arden's mouth left his and he lay back against the pillows, mutely inviting Leander to continue. Prompted by memories of the previous night, Leander's head lowered to Arden's cock and his tongue flicked over the head. A small sound of appreciation encouraged him, and he did it again. Remembering what Arden had done to him, Leander closed his lips softly around the very tip, swirling his tongue. Arden's hips lifted in reaction, and then his hands were in Leander's hair, stroking, long fingers caressing his scalp. Leander's stomach tightened at the touch, and he pushed his mouth down eagerly on Arden's cock, only to stop abruptly and pull back as it hit the back of his throat. He desperately tried to conquer his impulse to retch, thankful that his uncombed hair partially screened his face from Arden.

As he concentrated on regaining control of his breathing, he could hear the suppressed laughter in Arden's voice. "It's a skill that, like any other, requires practise, Leander."

Leander dared a glance at Arden's face. Arden's gaze was

filled with amusement, but as Leander stared up at the sensual face, he forgot his embarrassment and awkwardness. His mouth dried as he saw desire in the eyes that held his.

"And I suppose this is as good a time as any for me to practise." He tried, so very hard, to make it sound wry, to match Arden's mocking tones, but his words were breathless.

"Oh, most definitely," Arden agreed, settling more comfortably on his back, his legs parting slightly, letting Leander know precisely what he expected. This time Leander moved his mouth carefully down the shaft, finding out when he could take no more, and pulling back again to set up a rhythm. As he worked, he was gratified to hear Arden's sounds of pleasure and to feel the hands tightening in his hair. Arden was not as in control as his teasing comments implied. His tongue moved against the veined underside of Arden's cock and he sucked harder, his lips tight around the hot flesh as he stroked the heavy sac beneath. He could hear Arden's soft groans and, remembering what he had always hoped Bella or Caroline might do for him, he released the cock, glistening from his attentions, to mouth Arden's balls with soft lips, before gently drawing one and then the other into his mouth.

Hands in his hair pulled him abruptly away, up the bed and on top of Arden, Arden's tongue thrusting into his mouth as he rolled Leander over. After a cursory preparation with fingers and oil, Arden was pushing inside him. Leander's cry was drowned in the sound of satisfaction from Arden as his cock slid all the way inside Leander. Leander's head tilted back and he was gasping at the mixture of pain and pleasure. Arden's cock was too big, it hurt, he wanted it to stop, but he'd die if it did.

Arden began to thrust in a slow steady rhythm, lowering his head to bite at Leander's neck. Leander groaned as he felt Arden's size pushing into him. Arden was staring down now at Leander's face, his lips lifting back from his teeth as he thrust, his hair falling around his face in a dark curtain, face flushed as he drove mercilessly into Leander's arse until Leander cried out and his seed flooded over his skin. With a final series of hard thrusts and a hoarse cry, Arden came deep inside Leander.

Leander held Arden's sweat-slicked body against him, the unfamiliarity of the seed inside him tangible evidence of the pleasure that Arden took in him. Arden's head lowered to Leander's chest and licked at the seed there before his mouth descended on Leander's, compelling Leander to taste himself on Arden's tongue. Leander's eyes closed and he buried his hands in Arden's hair as he lost awareness of everything except Arden.

It was some time before Leander was recalled to reality, but when he was, it was in a distressing manner. Leander was about to follow Arden's example and arise from the bed when the clock on the mantelshelf struck the hour. The time that it struck was midday. He realised that Morris would by now have attended him in his room, and horror threatened to suffocate him.

"I must—my valet!" He pulled on his clothes with fingers that would not work properly. Arden said nothing as Leander tore the door open and raced along the corridor. Reaching the door to his bedchamber, he paused for an instant in a desperate prayer before opening it.

Morris wasn't there. There was no hot water or razor, no clothes were laid out, and the drapes were still drawn against the day outside.

Thankful beyond belief, he rumpled the undisturbed bed, opened the drapes, and then stood there, uncertain what he should do. He would not ring for Morris, for he was not yet ready to see anyone, but he knew that he must do something.

So he undressed, washed in cold water, and dressed once more. The familiar actions helped steady his breathing. Whatever madness had seized him the previous night, he had at least escaped detection.

Once he had finished, he sat in a chair and waited for Morris to bring his razor to him. As the minutes passed and the man still did not arrive, Leander could no longer hold back his thoughts.

He did not know, could not tell, how he had come to behave in such a way. He was no different from Arden or his friends. Leander had been observing them and thought they appeared to fall into two groups. There were those, like Hazell, who were past praying for, and those like Asbury, who appeared to wish only to shock their staid families by being an intimate of an infamous rake. Members of the latter group would drift away soon enough, their point made, and marry suitably. No doubt each would end his days as a father of a hopeful brood and weary his contemporaries by reminiscing interminably about his wild youth. Their place in Arden's following would be taken by other bored gentlemen seeking excitement.

Leander wondered how Arden would feel if he knew that he was viewed as a *divertissement* for the disaffected, sought out for the infamy that association with him would bring, rather than for himself. His lips twisted as he realised that Arden must know it. After all, he and he alone was responsible for the reputation he'd gained, and he did nothing to ameliorate it. Society's response could not be a surprise to the man.

Leander was uncertain how he fitted into the picture he had just painted of Arden and his circle of friends. He had no desire to shock. He had no particular desire to do anything that would draw attention to himself. But now . . . Did last night put him beyond redemption too? In the eyes of the *ton* it would, he did not doubt that. Yet being with Arden in such a way had been the first real pleasure he'd known since Bella's death. It had been unlike anything he had ever known. He shivered at the memory of that first kiss.

Selecting a neckcloth from those that Morris had unpacked, he tied it swiftly and without his usual care. No matter if it was not perfect — there was no one here who would be offended by casualness. A smile tugged at his mouth as he realised that, if Arden's actions last night had been characteristic, it was unlikely that the cravat would stay tied for long.

With that in mind, he picked up his pocket watch and reminded himself of the trick the jeweller had shown him of setting an alarm, which he hadn't done in all the time he had owned the watch. He'd sometimes thought himself foolish to spend so much on something that had intrigued him but for which he had no need. Although he could not be sure if he would require an alarm on the following morning, he hoped very much that he would.

"My lord!" Morris rushed into the room, startling Leander as much by his flustered manner as by the violence of his entrance. "I beg your pardon, my lord, but Mr Ferndean, His Grace's butler, wished for those of us who are visiting to attend a small celebration he was holding, and His Grace graciously provided some refreshment."

Morris stuttered to a halt before reaching an explanation of why this had caused his lack of punctuality. Looking at the state of the man, who was distinctly paler than usual and whose sparse brown hair did not appear to have seen the attentions of a comb that morning, Leander could infer the rest of the tale.

"In your politeness to our host, you were later to your bed than you had intended?" he suggested.

"Just so, my lord." Morris sounded more like his usual calm and controlled self.

"I have not long been from bed myself," Leander said,

unable to prevent a quick glance at his bed to ensure it looked realistically disturbed. "It is no matter. Now, where is my razor?"

He was about to untie his neckcloth, wondering just how lost in his thoughts he must have been to tie it before shaving, when his senses returned to him. He could not risk Morris seeing the marks that Arden had left on his neck. It burst in on him why Arden had arranged for the ladybirds to be present for this house party, for they provided cover to other activities. Yet, from the ladies he had known, Leander did not think one of the gentler sex was likely to bite him in passion, and so he dismissed Morris before removing his neckcloth. The man was still so overcome by his dereliction of duty — and his stale drunk — that he betrayed no surprise at the unusual order.

Once shaved and fully dressed, Leander glanced at himself in the looking glass before leaving his room. All his thoughts on the matter had led him to one conclusion — he was damned already, so he might as well enjoy it. With a heady rush of anticipation, Leander went in search of his lover.

Chapter Thirteen

The next few days were little short of an idyll, with Arden shamelessly neglecting his duty towards his other guests to spend time with Leander. Even during the relaxed evenings when the company gathered, Arden was rarely far from him for long. They could be at opposite ends of the room, but with one glance from Arden, Leander would feel the sudden heat of desire. Excusing himself to the group he was with, he would make his way towards Arden, who might or might not touch him as they left together.

Those were the times of desperate couplings, of biting and thrusting and needing and coming. Then there were the long nights spent in Arden's bed, lying in near-silence in the stillness of the night, touching and being touched, and mouths moving slowly over warm skin. There was the contentment of waking next to him each morning, and the freedom of the days, when nothing was planned and time was their own.

They rode out together on more than one occasion, over Arden's land and the surrounding countryside. Leander had been surprised on their first ride by the unmistakable signs of prosperity in the estate. Arden might have a reputation as a wastrel, but he evidently employed a good steward and did not begrudge him the means to keep the estate in order. Leander had also been surprised to find how well Arden knew the surrounding area. He had assumed that the man's time was spent in London in relentless pursuit of pleasure.

That Arden not only knew the locale but was a familiar figure in it was brought home to Leander on the fifth day, when they rode further afield than previously. They stopped at a village alehouse for refreshment, relinquishing their mounts into the hands of the boy who served as ostler. He stared wide-eyed at their rich clothes and highly bred horses until Leander, with a grin at the boy's unabashed wonder, flicked a shilling to him. That elicited a beaming, if grubby, smile and a recollection of his duty to their horses.

The landlord too stared in amazement as they entered the taproom. He evidently recognised Arden, bowing especially deeply to him as he welcomed the travellers. He bade them be seated, first wiping the wooden benches with his none-too-clean sleeve. Leander was intrigued by the way that, even while he spoke to them, his gaze darted around the empty room in what looked suspiciously like panic.

The reason for his worry soon became apparent. A voice from the doorway to the inner room of the alehouse reported that Ma had finished the ale and needed another immediately if she was to be kept from destroying the kitchen. The sound of smashing crockery appeared to bear out the statement. The owner of the voice was a lass of perhaps sixteen summers, her face framed by dusky ringlets, her dark-lashed eyes greenly wide as she gazed at the two gentlemen. When she bobbed a curtsey and smiled, two quite delectable dimples added to the charming picture of unspoiled beauty.

After one stricken look at Arden, the landlord hustled her back out through the doorway. A hissed "And *stay* there!" was heard before he returned.

"My apologies, Your Grace, your honour." Wiping his hands on his trousers, he glanced nervously at Arden.

Leander was biting his lip hard as Arden required two tankards of homebrew. He only dared meet Arden's eyes once the landlord had retreated.

Arden's eyebrows raised. "I have half a mind to venture into the kitchen," he remarked. "What do you say, Leander?"

Leander could no longer keep from laughing out loud. He was fully appreciative of the alarm and consternation that would surely result. As well let a fox loose in a hen house, except that this prey would no doubt go willingly to her fate.

"I should think that by now she will be locked in the cellar, only allowed out when you are a distant memory." He glanced at the rheumy-eyed decrepit who had evidently been hauled out of retirement and was slowly and carefully approaching with their drinks. "Or you could try your charms on our waiter instead," he urged, his voice low but alight with laughter. "They may yet sacrifice beauty in defence of age."

A brief laugh escaped Arden as he glanced in the direction Leander indicated before his gaze returned to Leander. He was suddenly intent, all amusement vanished as his eyes hungrily quartered Leander's laughing face.

"Or I could show them why such a prime article is presently safe from my depraved attentions," he murmured, leaning forward across the table. Leander felt his colour rise as he swayed towards Arden.

The moment was broken when the servitor placed the tankards down on the table with a muttered "Your honours."

Arden glanced irritably at him as he stood there waiting. "Well?"

"Would your honours like anything to eat?" he offered with a nervous bob of his head. "Mrs Day has cooked up some pigs' trotters, and there is curd pudding and — "

Seeing the look on Arden's face, Leander swiftly raised his hand to break off the recital. "Thank you, but we are not hungry."

A bob of the head, and they were left in peace. "No appetite, Leander?" Arden questioned, his leg curving around Leander's beneath the table. Leander's mouth was dry as he stared into dark, intent eyes. "I shall remind you of that."

Arden looked away finally, and the spell was broken.

Leander raised the tankard to his mouth, trying not to think of pouring rich red wine over Arden's gloriously naked body and slowly licking it off.

They didn't linger, staying just time enough for the horses to be watered and for Ma to demand, courtesy of the aged servitor this time, another tankard of ale. As the man made his painfully slow way towards the kitchen, the crashing of crockery signalled Ma's disapproval of the delay. Arden and Leander met one another's eyes in silent agreement and rose to leave.

They were scarcely out of sight of the last house of the village, in the shelter of a copse, when Arden abruptly swerved his horse close against Leander's mount. He curved his hand around the back of Leander's neck to pull him across for a fierce kiss. By the time he released Leander's mouth, Leander was breathing hard. He saw Arden swing off his horse and instantly dismounted his own animal.

Arden impatiently divested himself of his close-fitting coat before turning his attention to stripping Leander of his. He did not stop at the coat—Leander's cravat, waistcoat, and shirt swiftly came to adorn the grass, and Arden's busy hands frustrated Leander's every attempt to reciprocate. Arden unfastened his own breeches and withdrew the familiar small bottle from his pocket. Leander saw no more, for Arden spun him around, pushed him face-first against the nearest tree, and yanked his breeches down. The oil bottle fell unheeded to the grass as Arden slid his fingers into Leander, working him swiftly and urgently, and then his cock was pushing in.

Leander cried out, and Arden withdrew slightly, only to push back in, again and again. His forceful thrusts drove Leander against the oak's rough bark until his face was torn and it was only the strength with which his arms were braced that prevented the same treatment from being delivered to his cock. As Arden thrust into him, Leander cried out again, pushing back, demanding to be fucked harder, until Arden buried his mouth in his neck as his hips pumped into Leander.

Breathing in gasps, Arden withdrew and relaxed his hold on Leander. Desperate to come himself, Leander turned and reached for him. Arden moved back a step, his hand on Leander's hip pushing him backwards.

"Kneel down, Leander." Arden's voice was ragged, and his chest rose and fell swiftly.

His gaze holding Arden's, breathing fast, Leander knelt on the springy turf before him.

Arden stood looking at him. "Hands and knees."

His heart pounding, his cock almost hurting, Leander did as he was told. Arden moved around behind him and pulled his breeches further down. Leander jerked forward suddenly, crying out as a warm tongue probed between the cheeks of his arse. He moaned and pushed back again, gasping at the feel of Arden's tongue snaking over his skin. He trembled as he felt the warmth and cried out as it pushed inside, probing and quivering within him. He would have begged Arden to touch his cock, but couldn't find the words. His desperate cries filled the summer afternoon in a wordless pleading.

Arden's attentions suddenly stopped. Leander was left alone, the only sounds those of the horses tearing at the grass, their bits chinking, and Arden's boots moving a few steps over the turf. He turned his head as Arden came back to him, and his eyes widened as he saw Arden held his riding whip.

His mind protested perversion, but before he could move, Arden was kneeling in front of him, his mouth covering Leander's and his tongue pushing in. Arden's kiss was a painful reminder of his need and he whimpered into Arden's mouth. He was left empty as Arden pulled back, offering Leander his finger instead. Leander's eyes closed as he sucked it, readying it to slide inside him and bring him to exquisite release. When

Arden withdrew his finger, Leander made a sound of need and reached after it with his mouth. Instead, something thicker and harder pressed against his lips.

His eyes snapped open to find it was the wide tip of the whip's leather handle. He froze. But Arden's hand was in his hair, long fingers caressing his scalp as he gently worked the broad head between Leander's lips in a rhythm so familiar that it was not long before his mouth was eagerly moving up and down on the braided leather, his tongue exploring the woven texture of the shaft before he sucked it, desperate for stimulation, desperate to come. He protested the whip's eventual withdrawal, and Arden held it before him for an instant. He kissed it and heard Arden's indrawn breath.

Then Arden was standing, moving around him, and the anticipation was almost unbearable as he felt the wide head of the whip against his arse. He gasped as it began to move inside him, pushing and stretching him until his trembling arms gave way and his cheek was pressed against the grass. His breath came in sobs and he pushed back steadily against the incredible pressure. It stopped at last, and he groaned, only to cry out as Arden pulled it slowly back and pushed in again.

"You're a whore, Leander — your legs spread wider than a Haymarket harlot, begging for this."

His mouth opened to furiously deny Arden's stinging comment, but the only sound to come out was a long groan as Arden started to work the whip inside him.

"You'll do anything I want, won't you? And love it."

He bit hard at his hand to contain the sounds, but Arden's vicious commentary was exciting him almost as much as the fullness inside him and he was helpless to prevent his guttural animal noises as Arden worked the whip harder.

"What would they all say if they saw you now, loving it like this?" He pushed it deeper and Leander whimpered.

"What would your brother think, Leander, if he saw you now, your cock so hard and heavy and desperate, wet with your excitement?"

Leander heard no more through his cries as Arden slid the whip in and out of him. All he knew was his desperate need to come as Arden fucked him with the handle of his whip. Seeing suddenly how it must look, how *Arden* must look, Leander's scream ripped his throat raw as he came.

Afterwards, he collapsed bonelessly onto the turf, vaguely aware that Arden was removing the whip and sliding inside Leander himself. A few thrusts were all that was necessary, and then Arden gasped out his pleasure.

Arden's weight slumping on him afterwards threatened to crush him, but Leander didn't want him to move. He could feel Arden's chest rising and falling almost as hard as his own, his harsh breathing in Leander's ear pausing only when he kissed Leander's damp neck and murmured his name. Leander's eyes closed in true contentment. Arden had never before done such a thing. He could want for no greater happiness than this.

Before their breathing had steadied, Arden rolled off him. Leander turned over to find the man already getting to his feet and adjusting his clothing. Leander followed suit slowly, far from recovered still, trying to subdue his urge to grin at Arden like a particularly moon-kissed village idiot. He was still making himself decent when Arden mounted his horse.

"For God's sake, Ockley, don't be so dilatory," he demanded impatiently.

Leander looked up in surprise to find Arden already riding away. Grabbing his horse's reins to prevent it from following its fellow, Leander paused to pull on his coat, then mounted and followed Arden. He found he was more comfortable standing unobtrusively in his stirrups than committing himself to the saddle.

The ride back to the house was inexplicably awkward. Leander attempted a couple of conversational openings, but when they were ignored, he retreated uncertainly into silence. He had no idea what had caused this sudden change in Arden's mood.

Upon their return, Arden absented himself with no explanation, leaving Leander to his own devices. Bewildered, he took refuge in a bath, feeling the sting of warm water where the tree's rough bark had scraped his chest and face. He thought back as he sat in the cooling water, trying to understand what had changed Arden's mood, to see if he might in some manner have caused offence, but an explanation eluded him.

He remained none the wiser as Arden ignored his presence at dinner that night and the gaming table thereafter. As a result, Leander spent much of the evening with Broughton, gleaning from him news about the war with which his brother had neglected to provide him. At some point in the early hours, he looked up from their conversation to find that Arden, and many others, had already retired for the night.

Leander excused himself from Broughton and made his way to Arden's room. He paused at the closed door. For the first time, he wondered if he would be welcome. Annoyance spurred him into action. To be reduced to hovering uncertainly, like some schoolroom miss at her debut, was intolerable. He pushed the door open and walked in.

Arden wasn't there. Leander stood stunned before his brain began to take in the corollary of this. Or the *possible* corollary, he told himself. He had no reason to suspect that Arden was satisfying his desire elsewhere. He was undoubtedly engaged in an interesting conversation, loath for it to end.

Leander returned to his own chamber, where he stripped off somewhat jerkily and climbed into bed, blowing out the candle. He lay in the dark, every sense strained for a sound that would tell him of Arden's approach. Eventually, he fell asleep.

He woke alone the following morning. Fighting the bleakness that threatened to engulf him, Leander lay in bed until his valet arrived.

He had dismissed Morris and was about to proceed downstairs for breakfast when Arden strode in. He was dressed only in shirt and pantaloons, his hair loose and curling over his broad shoulders.

Leander's temper flared at the man's arrogant behaviour. "What the devil do you think you're playing at, Arden?"

Arden's burning eyes met Leander's. "Your meaning?"

"If you find my presence irksome, I suggest you tell me so that I may remove myself." Leander spat the words angrily.

Arden's nostrils flared. "You will leave when I tell you and not before."

Leander held that arrogant gaze for an instant longer before he strode towards the door. Hell and the devil take it, the man was conceited.

Arden's hand bit into his arm and swung him round. Tearing his arm out of the man's grip, he glared at Arden. He had no warning as Arden lunged at him, driving him backwards to the floor and crashing on top of him. Leander's breath was driven from his body, and Arden's heavy blow split his lip. Leander clouted the side of Arden's head and tried to shift the man above him, all science forgotten in his anger as he and Arden wrestled for supremacy.

They reached an impasse, both breathing heavily, furious eyes holding. Then, with a move so swift Leander had no time to avoid it, Arden's mouth descended on Leander's and he began to tear Leander's clothes open. Arden found Leander's nipple and tweaked it with his fingers, causing him to arch upwards, cursing and no longer wishing to fight.

Leander was still swearing when Arden started fucking him, but now he was demanding more, faster, needing to feel Arden deep inside him. Leander's oaths intensified as Arden brought them both to completion

They lay slumped on the carpet afterwards, the only thing to break the silence the sound of their laboured breathing. After a while, Arden climbed to his feet and offered his hand to help Leander up. He looked over the ruin of Leander's clothing, then down at himself, and his lips lifted slightly.

"A change of clothing may be in order before we venture into the public gaze."

Rubbing the back of his hand across his bleeding lip, Leander agreed. His eyes were on Arden still, awaiting some sort of explanation.

None was forthcoming. Arden offered no reason for his absence or for his reaction this morning. Leander would have pursued it, but somehow the knowledge that all was back to how it had been seemed to be more important than questioning what had happened and risking a repetition of Arden's removal from his company. Leander said nothing.

Chapter Fourteen

The days that followed saw a return to Leander's idyll. He thrust from himself any thought of the night of desertion and enjoyed every moment of Arden's favour that was his. It seemed that it filled each waking hour. There were times, too, when Leander roused briefly in the night to find Arden's arm flung possessively across him and heard Arden's breathing, slow and deep in sleep, change slightly as Leander moved closer against him.

On his way to change for dinner late one afternoon, Leander was stopped by the butler. "My lord, a letter has arrived for you."

Surprised, Leander took it from him. A swift glance was sufficient to inform him of the sender's identity, for the scrawl of the direction was one with which he was all too familiar. Henry's style of letter-writing was unparalleled. He usually contrived to manage at least four laborious lines of news to his brother before the subject turned candidly to his shortage of funds and the expenses incurred by an officer in His Majesty's army. As Leander broke the seal and scanned the single sheet, his ironic smile faded, and his hand tightened convulsively on the letter.

"Tell my man to make ready to leave immediately," he ordered the butler, turning to take the stairs two at a time. He found Arden in his dressing room, removing his cravat as he began to change for dinner.

"I have to leave," he blurted out. "My mother is taken ill. I must return to town immediately."

Arden shot a keen glance at him, then unfastened his shirt. "I see. And what, may I ask, afflicts her?"

Leander realised he did not have that information. He raised the crumpled sheet to read it through again. "I don't know precisely. Henry does not say."

"It's your brother who writes to you, then."

"What does that matter? My man will pack my belongings directly. My apologies, Arden, but I must depart immediately."

Lost in calculating the distance he could cover before daylight was gone, Leander did not notice Arden's approach until the touch on his cheek brought him back to his surroundings.

"I find it decidedly odd," Arden murmured, as he began to untie Leander's cravat, "that your mother who was, I understand, in perfect health but ten days since, should find herself afflicted by a mysterious illness that demands your instant return to town. An illness that, moreover, carries no apparent symptoms. If I had a distrustful mind, I might wonder at the timing of your brother's missive."

Leander stared uncomprehendingly for an instant before he knocked Arden's hand aside with a curse. "Damn you, Arden—do you think this some sort of game?"

Fury blazed in Arden's eyes, matched by the clear anger that burned in Leander as he glared back. Arden's rage seemed slowly to dim as he looked at Leander.

"Come, Leander," he said at last, with the hint of a persuasive smile, "Your brother doesn't exactly approve of me." His hand moved across Leander's arse and pulled him close. Leander's cock reacted to the feel of Arden pressing against him, protesting at the sudden tightness of his buckskin breeches. Arden's long fingers swiftly unbuttoned them before he knelt before Leander, looking up at him, rendering him unable to think of anything except Arden.

"Perhaps he thinks I'll corrupt you," he said. Then he pushed his mouth down on Leander's cock, taking it deep inside. At the tightness and the pressure around him, Leander's hands wrapped in Arden's hair and he bit down into his lip in an attempt not to scream out his pleasure. Arden's hands ran over his arse before tugging his breeches down. As a finger investigated further, Leander almost lost control. Arden pulled away from him, leaving him to gasp his disappointment.

He let Arden order him as he chose, allowing himself to be bent over the back of a chair, oiled fingers pushing deep inside him until he was moaning his need for Arden. The damp head of Arden's cock pressed against him. Leander moaned again and pushed back in desperate invitation.

"Please," he said, his voice thick with need as he heard flesh against flesh, knowing Arden was rubbing his oiled hand over his cock.

"*Please*," he begged when the sounds stopped and nothing further happened.

He felt the tip of Arden's cock as Arden thrust slightly with his hips, then stilled again.

"So, Leander, do you think this is what your brother is worried about?"

The words took a moment to penetrate his lust-fogged brain. "I have no doubt you're right," he said with a choke of laughter as he imagined Henry finding out that his dully dutiful brother had been bent over an example of Chippendale's better work with the Duke of Arden's cock in his arse.

Arden reached around and began to run a finger over the head of Leander's cock. "I cannot help but think that to return to London at his behest will only increase his determination to control you for his own advantage. Don't you?"

As he finished speaking, Arden slid all the way inside Leander, leaving him crying out incoherently, his eyes closing in the unbelievable pleasure of feeling Arden inside him. Arden established a rhythm, his hand around Leander's cock so that every thrust of his hips sent it sliding through the tightness of his hand.

"Stay, Leander," he said, his hips stilling suddenly.

Leander bent over even further, offering himself. But Arden made no move.

"Stay," Arden said again.

Leander's eyes opened. "I can't," he said at last. "I must go — she needs me."

His eyes closed again as he felt Arden withdraw from him. "Go then."

Disbelieving, he straightened up and saw Arden walking towards the door, his breeches held together with a careless hand as he looked out into the corridor.

"You," he said. "Find Farraday and bring him here."

He turned back into the room, his eyes glancing disinterestedly over Leander.

Leander was struggling with his breeches, pulling them up. "Arden," he started.

Arden opened one of the drawers in his dressing table and lifted from it something made of leather and chain. Leander couldn't identify it but thought it looked not unlike a piece of harness.

"Arden," he said again.

"What?" Arden's voice was cool and bored as he walked into his bedroom.

Leander stood in the doorway, hesitating. He wanted to explain that he didn't want to go, that he had no choice, but the coldness in Arden kept him silent. He turned away, finding it easy to fasten his breeches over his softening cock. With renewed resolve he turned back, only to find that Arden was lying on his bed, his breeches still open and his cock standing forth, dark and hard. Leander swallowed. He moved towards the bed, but as he did so, Farraday strode in, Hazell close upon his heels.

"Richard wanted to come too, Arden. I hope you don't mind." Farraday was hesitant.

Arden's eyes glittered as they passed over Leander and met Farraday's gaze. "Why should I mind?" he enquired off-handedly. "You can bring me to release between you."

Farraday became aware of Leander's presence and his eyes moved between Leander and Arden in ill-disguised speculation. A knowing smile dawned on Hazell's face as he looked at the discomfited earl. Leander turned abruptly and left.

He'd covered no more than ten miles before dusk forced him to stop at an inn. There was no moon, these roads were unfamiliar to him, and any accident would delay him longer than a night spent at a hostelry. He knew from Morris's demeanour that the man thought him mad not to have waited until the following day to begin his journey, but he couldn't have spent another minute there, let alone another night.

He left his equipage to the ostler. As he strode across the courtyard to the inn, his bootheels struck the cobbles in a way that would have indicated to any who knew Leander that it might be advisable to avoid him for a time. Leander did not often allow his temper full rein, but when he did, the results tended to be spectacular.

The innkeeper had been flustered by Morris's demand for a room for his master. When Leander entered, he was apologising fulsomely, mortified to the depths of his soul, for the fact that the private parlour was currently undergoing extensive renovation. There had been an unfortunate incident involving well-lubricated young officers on leave from the Peninsula and the room was no longer fit to be offered to the esteemed customer. The meal he could offer was also below the standard he would wish.

Leander disclaimed any desire for a private parlour, a meal, or anything save a bottle of claret that he would take in his room. He was shown to the best chamber of the modest inn, one that might be described by those uncharitably inclined as poky. Leander scarcely noticed as he sat in the only seat the small room offered and made steady inroads on the claret, the quality of which was no more than might be expected from an inn of this size.

He would not think of his mother, of how seriously ill she might be, and how she would be looking for his arrival while he was forced to wait here until daylight. Pouring himself another glass of wine, he faced the unwelcome truth that he was powerless to do anything that night.

Attempting to redirect his thoughts, he untied his cravat by the light of the tallow candles. He had dispensed with Morris's services that night, needing to be alone. His eyes in the looking glass grew dark as he realised that he had dispensed with his valet's services for the last several evenings. Arden and he had undressed one another each night, either ripping off their clothes in desperate need, or removing them slowly, mouths searching over the gradually uncovered flesh until their clothes were a disordered heap on the floor and they lay entwined on Arden's bed, moving together in languorous desire.

He picked up his glass and tossed back the contents. The rough wine burned his throat as he remembered the addictive pleasure of those long nights when the only things that mattered were the warmth of Arden's body, the velvet of his voice, the delight of his caress, and the certainty that he wanted Leander.

Slamming the glass down, he threw his cravat aside. There was no point in remembering. It was over. He might think it all a dream were it not for the grazes on his face where Arden had taken him against the tree. They were fading fast enough and would soon be completely vanished. Whatever madness had taken hold of him had gone, never to return. Arden had left no doubt that Leander's place in his bed would be — indeed, already had been — easily filled.

Given that was the case, Leander decided, what had happened between them when he left was for the best. Arden had made it painfully clear that Leander's decision to leave did not trouble him in any way. Leander had merely been the latest diversion, interesting only because of his novelty, discarded as soon as that was gone. Take the night when Arden disappeared. He must have already grown bored with Leander. Why he had come back to him afterwards remained something of a mystery, however.

Leander groaned and dropped his head into his hands as full realisation dawned on him. There could be only one explanation for that. Arden had come back to Leander because of what he symbolised to Arden. He had been a dutiful, proper member of the *ton* who had been willing, so very willing, to be corrupted. There was still satisfaction to be gained by Arden in the knowledge that the hitherto respectable Earl of Ockley behaved no differently than a bitch in heat. Look at the way he had told Leander as much when he'd used his whip.

Leander's fists clenched against his forehead at the memory of his shameless depravity and Arden's scorn of it, even then. Arden would have found immense gratification in keeping Leander on his hook until they returned to London, where the whole *ton* would have witnessed his laughable obsession with Arden, his eagerness to do anything Arden wanted of him.

Leander's head began to ache. He had been precisely what Henry had accused him of being when he first met Arden — an innocent at large. Worse, an innocent who had welcomed the excitement of corruption, mistaking it for freedom. He deserved to be whipped for his stupidity. How Arden must have exulted each time Leander had begged for his cock. He must have delighted in the wantonness that Leander had discovered lay within himself, not caring how Arden used him, only that he did. And how he must have revelled when Leander initiated their encounters, as he had frequently done. Leander's stomach churned. Arden's friends would be entertained for months to come with stories of the gullible earl's eagerness and desperation. It was not only the fact of his depravity and need that would become common currency within Arden's set but also the extent of it.

Leander sat in the dingy room while the evening's business went on downstairs. Sounds of drunken jokes and raucous laughter echoed through the inn. As the night wore on, the noises gradually quietened. He could hear the last customers leaving, the landlord locking up downstairs, and then heavy footsteps as he came up to his own room.

Moving stiffly, Leander rose from his chair to undress. He blew out the candles and climbed between cold sheets. He lay with his eyes open in the darkness, staring blindly at the ceiling.

Chapter Fifteen

Leander was up at dawn, setting off shortly thereafter without stopping to break his fast. He was filled with fear for his mother and pushed the horses hard. Henry had not intimated that the case was desperate, but he would scarcely have written to his brother were it not serious.

By the time he drew up in Green Street, his set face and the frown between his eyes owed as much to anxiety as tiredness.

"My lord!" Pickett was uncharacteristically startled when Leander burst into the hall. "We did not know to expect your return," he continued, but Leander ignored him, taking the stairs two at a time.

Striding along the landing to the next flight, he stopped as he saw Henry descending. "How is she?" he asked urgently.

Henry made an instant quieting gesture, which did nothing to calm his worst imaginings. He steered them into the drawing room, closing the door behind them.

"Lea," he started, as Leander stripped off his gloves. "The thing is . . ."

"What?" Leander snapped as Henry trailed off. "Tell me the worst, Henry."

Henry moistened his lips. "She's improved since I wrote to you," he said at last.

Leander drew a breath of relief. Anticipating his next question, Henry added, "She's resting."

"What ails her?" Leander asked more quietly, removing his travel-stained coat and placing it on the nearest chair before seating himself. "What does Cooper say?"

114

Henry remained standing. "She hasn't seen him."

Leander's brows slammed together. "Hasn't seen him?" he echoed. "Devil take it, he's one of the few leeches worth consulting! I'll call him in even if she doesn't want it."

"It's not necessary. She's almost recovered," Henry insisted.

Leander looked uncomprehendingly at his brother. "Recovered? Yet it was only two days ago that she was ill enough . . ." Leander didn't finish his sentence. His mind filled with suspicion as he stared at his increasingly uneasy brother. "Has Mama actually been ill at all?" he enquired in a dangerously soft voice.

"Yes!" It burst from Henry in indignation. "She's been sick with apprehension since you left, in fear that someone might find out where you had gone and ask her about it. And Thomas and I have been recalled from next month, so now she is cast into dejection too and has taken to her bed with a sick headache." He eyed the wrath on Leander's face. "Damn it, Lea, don't come high and mighty with me. She's been cast into the fidgets and hasn't been eating, and I thought if you were back, it would at least relieve her mind of one anxiety."

Leander remained seated. If he were to stand, he knew he would surely kill his brother. "You dragged me back here under false pretences, careless of the anxiety your letter caused, when all along she suffered from nothing more than megrims. You wanted my return because it suited your purposes. Worse, you don't scruple to use Mama in that way?"

"You misrepresent the situation," Henry objected, his face stubborn. "Everyone knows of the depraved nature of Arden's gatherings, and if people were to discover you were party to them . . . You might not care about your reputation, Lea, but you should think of Mama."

"As *you* do when you're with Burnage," Leander said, his anger rising still further. "For God's sake, Henry, don't play self-righteous with me. You don't give a damn about me or my reputation. All you care about is yourself."

"That's not true." Henry looked hurt.

Leander's eyes closed briefly. He would still happily see his brother's bleeding corpse at his feet, but he couldn't ignore that Henry had, for once, been right. Leander had thought the risk of a little social disfavour worthwhile when he'd believed that he and Arden—But what he had so joyously embraced had been a chimera, conjured by the man's delight in mockery and his own desperate need. Left with nothing to show for his gullibility save searing humiliation, Leander hoped desperately that knowledge of his involvement in one of Arden's infamous house parties would not become common currency among the *ton*.

He rose slowly to his feet. "While I abominate your methods, your intentions were good."

He held out his hand to his brother. Henry, looking startled but pleased, shook it. Leander had turned away, ready to retire to his room and tidy himself after the long drive, when the door to the drawing room opened.

"Leander!" With a cry of delight, his mama flung herself into his arms. "Leander, you can have no idea how glad I am to see you. We have missed you so, haven't we, Henry? And to know you must be having such a horrid time with that man and his awful friends quite overset me. Henry will tell you that I have not been myself all the time you were gone. But now you are back in time for the Beaumonts' assembly tomorrow night, and I have the most ravishing new gown you have ever seen, and Sir John will be present, and—Leander! What has happened to your face?"

Puzzled when the dowager's dainty hand reached to his cheek, Leander's face heated as he realised. "A branch caught me as I was riding," he supplied swiftly, aware of Henry's eyes on him.

116

"Oh Leander, you haven't changed, have you? You were so clumsy as a child, not at all like dear Henry. You would have thought by now you would have learned not to hurt yourself so. Now, come." She tugged determinedly at her eldest son's arm. "You must sit with me. Henry, come and sit beside me too. I wish to hear what your plans are for the next week, for there is still time, you know, to make an offer for Annabel Sedgewick before you return to Spain."

Leander sat obediently where he was bidden and arranged his face into an expression of polite interest. There could be no doubt that he was home.

Leander spent the following morning in his book room, working through the papers and bills that had collected during his absence. The concentration they required allowed him to forget the disjointed dreams he'd suffered, waking to find time after time that he was alone, to remember time after time that, in full knowledge of what he was doing, of what the man was, he had gone gladly to Arden's bed. His stomach had twisted as he realised he would still be there were it not for Henry's subterfuge. He would still be wretchedly loving every second he spent with Arden, unaware that the man was merely amusing himself at Leander's expense, his only purpose the lure of Leander's disgrace.

He had been relieved when the hour was sufficiently advanced for him to rise. Leander had joined his mother at the breakfast table and steeled himself to accompany her to the Beaumonts' that night as she so gaily assumed he would.

Leander was frowning at the papers before him, unable to concentrate fully upon them. He looked up as the door to the book room opened and his brother entered.

Henry was not here for small talk. "Stories are circulating about you and Arden."

Leander's heart stopped, then began to pound. "Indeed?"

he asked, forcing calm into his voice. "And you listen to gossip, do you, Henry?"

"This is serious, Lea. They're saying that you and Arden — that you went to his bed."

The pulse in his head was hammering. "My private life is no concern of yours."

"Your private life may not be, but this is no longer private." Henry ranged himself in front of the fireplace and looked his brother over. "I know you did as they're saying — I saw your expression yesterday when Mama asked about your face, although how that happened, God only knows. But it's why you went to stay with him in the first place, isn't it? Lea, I *told* you —"

Leander was on his feet. "Is this offensive speculation leading anywhere?"

Henry glared at his brother. "Will you stop being so damned condescending and listen to what I have to say? I want to help. I don't want the family name besmirched."

Leander sank back into his chair. He was almost trembling. "What can I do, Henry?" he asked quietly. "It's true. What can I do?"

"Do you intend to continue the association with Arden?" Henry's tone was hard.

Leander winced. "God, no."

That won an approving nod from his brother. "The true nature of your liaison with Arden is known only amongst those of us who — well, those like us, and we guard our own. You may rest easy on that front. The rest of the *ton* know of the opera dancers who attended and will believe you have become a depraved libertine, partaking in drunken orgies. You must hope they do not also believe you involved in further degradation, if the tales of his vile devilry are true."

"Devilry?" Leander echoed, confused. "He is indeed all that is debauched and —" He stopped, for the charge of villainy he had been about to lay against the man was unmerited. Arden had brought Leander to the point of begging, but everything Leander had done, the choices he had made, had been of his own volition. Leander could not claim, even to himself, that he had been coerced in any way. Therein lay the cruelty of the man.

"There is talk that he furthers the legacy of the Medmenham Monks." Henry lowered his voice even though they were alone. "It is said there are secret caves at his estate where hellfire rages on the Sabbath, and he has dark altars on which young maidens are violated before he ends their lives."

Despite his misery, laughter bubbled up inside Leander. It was preposterous to think of Arden taking anything seriously enough, whether it be worship of the devil or mockery of the church, to dress in robes and conduct rites as those of the Hellfire Club had done. As for Arden murdering ladybirds who might more usefully have been occupied in pleasuring him, the idea was positively farcical.

"Regardless of the details, the *ton* believe him beyond redemption," Henry said swiftly, perhaps having seen his brother's incredulity. "That you have spent time as his guest is bad enough for Mama to live with. Thomas says you must continue as usual and pretend not to notice any gossip, and they will forget the association in time. The worst thing you can do is hide."

Smarting from the realisation that Henry and Burnage had discussed his situation and that they obviously thought him too stupid to work out the need to continue in his usual way, Leander held his tongue. Henry meant well.

Henry's gaze rested on Leander's face. "Why'd you do it? I don't understand."

Leander shook his head, unable to answer. He still did not comprehend the madness that had driven him to behaviour he now regretted fiercely. "I don't know," he said at last, his voice almost inaudible.

"Damned stupidity, anyway," Henry said. "I lay odds that Annesley won't have you for his daughter now."

The clear conviction dawned on Leander. "That's what all this is about, isn't it?" For some reason, the comprehension hurt him. "That's why you want to help—so that my name isn't sullied beyond what a respectable family would tolerate in their son-in-law. You don't want me to spoil my chances of getting wed and producing an heir. That's your only concern in all this, isn't it?"

"Actually, it's not. But as you evidently think so little of me, I'll take my leave. Glad I'm going back to Spain is all I can say," Henry added, lounging towards the door. "At least there I won't have to listen to everyone animadverting on my brother's iniquity."

The door slammed behind him, leaving Leander to his bitter reflections.

CHAPTER SIXTEEN

L eander regarded himself in the looking glass, noting with relief that the abrasions on his face were now all but invisible. He was pale, however, and lines of tension bracketed his jaw. He could not be sure whether these were from the anticipation of what was to come this evening or left over from his unpleasant interview with his mother.

Knowing it to be only a matter of time before Henry tattled to her, he had broken the news himself. He told her nothing of the substance of the rumours, merely that his stay with Arden had become common knowledge. Her face had turned white, and he had to send for her maid to bring her vinaigrette. It was some time before she recovered enough to do more than moan softly.

"I *knew* you shouldn't have gone," she lamented. "I *told* you, Leander. Why won't you *listen* to your mother?" She broke off to open her vinaigrette again, and then her eyes raised with disconcerting steadiness to his. "Why *did* you stay with him?"

Leander realised that she wanted an answer. This, to her, was the least comprehensible part of the whole damnable mess—that her son should seek out the company of an avowed degenerate. Forced to confront his reasons, Leander at length confessed the truth. "I liked him." He shrugged helplessly, remembering. "I thought we were friends."

His mother wailed as awareness of a new disaster dawned on her. "And how can I face dear Lady Annesley? She trusted you with Sophia and allowed you liberties in conversing with her, you know. Now she will think you nothing more than a hardened *rake!*"

The conversation had continued along similar lines until the dowager had finally declared herself exhausted and had herself put to bed. She was too overcome to attend the Beaumonts' assembly tonight — to which she had been looking forward for an *age* — and she sincerely hoped that she was not too ill to sleep. It was only in sleep that she would be able to forget her son's behaviour.

At least that meant that Leander was going to the Beaumonts' alone. If there were to be gossip, his mother would not suffer it at first hand. He had dressed for the assembly with more than usual care. His clothes were of their accustomed sobriety, but he wore a fob and a ring in a gesture of appeasement towards fashion. He would give society nothing with which to reproach him there. He glanced at the brown diamond set into the ring, remembering when Bella had given it to him. She had been excited about finding something special for him, insisting that the colour reflected that of his eyes. It had taken all his self-control not to question her giddy anticipation until she'd been ready to surprise him with the gift. Everything then had been so simple. His heart was heavy as he left to face the verdict of the *ton*.

Leander timed his arrival so that the evening's entertainment would be well advanced and those whom he counted among his friends already present. He wished to make his entrance as unobtrusively as possible before swiftly joining a welcoming group.

The room did not precisely fall silent when he arrived, but he was aware he was attracting attention. Curious stares seemed to survey him from every direction as he waited for his hostess to greet him. Lady Beaumont appeared not to have noticed his arrival. That must be an oversight — she would be busy tonight. He looked around for one of his friends, for someone with whom he might converse, fighting down the beginnings of panic as acquaintance after acquaintance seemed not to notice his presence. By the time his gaze fell on Percy Stanford, a gentleman from White's with whom he dined on a regular basis, he knew a sense of indescribable relief. Attempting a smile at Stanford, he moved towards him. Stanford looked straight through him before turning his back.

Leander stopped dead. The dancing and the conversations were still progressing as usual, but he felt he was the centre of all attention. He moistened his dry lips. To leave now would be to ensure that never again could he show his face in society. Yet how could he stay when there was no one who would recognise him?

He turned around once more, searching. None of the mamas who had been so assiduous in their invitations to him when they sought a rich husband for their daughters, none of his acquaintances from White's, not one of them would hold his gaze.

His head held high, Leander prepared to walk out of the ballroom.

"Ockley! There you are, at last!"

He turned, startled, at the loud voice. Sir John Gillingham was jostling people in his rush to reach Leander.

"Come, tell me all. I have heard such wild tales about an unseasonable house party and the dashing young blades who attended, but I believe it was all a hum and that you were instead inspecting racehorses for the next meeting at Epsom."

Sir John threw a casual arm across his shoulders when he reached him, his head bent close to catch Leander's answer.

"I'm sure you are correct," Leander managed between bloodless lips.

A brief squeeze of his shoulder, so brief that he was not sure if he had imagined it, and then Sir John's voice boomed out again, at a volume a little too great to be polite. "Linton,

Ockley is being most close-mouthed. Can you persuade him to take us into his confidence?"

The flash of fury in Lord Linton's face betrayed his realisation of Sir John's shameless methods. Refuse to acknowledge Leander, and Sir John would no doubt ask whether his youngest son, whose involvement with Arden's set the peer tried to keep quiet, had yet returned from the house party. Leander could see little of Farraday in his father as he bestowed a false smile upon Leander and laughed awkwardly.

"Oh, I don't doubt that Lord Ockley's horse will win the Derby this year," he said.

"Deuced unfair, I call it," Sir John agreed, as Linton turned away again. "Don't you agree, Linton?"

Realising he was not going to be released so easily, Linton swung back round. "How is your brother?" he bit out in Leander's direction, his eyes still furious. "The Frenchies must be glad to see him still in England."

"As we all are," Leander agreed, his face stiff. "I am not sure quite when he and Captain Burnage return, but it will be a sad loss to us."

"Ringrose tells me that his son is due to return home shortly," Linton continued, evidently unwilling to bear the burden alone any longer.

Ringrose, ever eager to talk of his son's military career, needed no persuading. A full half hour had passed before his enthusiasm began to wane. By that time, Jack Sittingbourne and his wife had arrived. After seeing his wife comfortably established, Jack swiftly made his way to Leander and stayed talking to him for some considerable time. At some point during their conversation, those present seemed to realise they had been victims of a most improper joke, for no one could suspect depravity from the Earl of Ockley, of all men!

Lady Beaumont finally took the plunge. "Lord Ockley," she trilled, detaching him from Jack. "I am so sorry I missed you when you arrived. Lady Emilia was a trifle overcome by the heat. But I see you have not yet engaged yourself to dance. May I introduce you to a partner?"

Before Leander could frame a diplomatic refusal—the last thing he could afford to do was put himself in a position where he might be publicly rejected—Lady Beaumont, with the air of one extracting a rabbit from a hat, triumphantly produced her daughter Lady Charlotte.

Almost before he knew it, Leander was following the familiar moves of the cotillion with Lady Charlotte, noting a curious look in her eyes as he did so. He wondered if her mama had placed her under duress to dance with him. It was only when she held his hand for an instant too long that he recognised the expression for what it was—excitement. She would not know the details, of course, but she must have apprehended something of Leander's disgrace, and her grey eyes held a thrill of illicit pleasure each time she looked at him.

Returning her to her mama as soon as was decent, he saw the triumph in Lady Beaumont's face. She thought she had carried the day by seizing the advantage in such a manner. She was not to labour under this misapprehension for long. Lady Annesley bore down inexorably upon him, the obedient Sophia in her wake.

He forced a smile, seeing the peculiar mixture of speculation and distaste in Lady Annesley's face as she greeted him. It seemed that she did not know what to believe, yet she would not risk losing the best prize on the marriage mart if no one else gave credence to the rumours. She proceeded to proffer her daughter before him like a ripe apple before a horse.

Sophia was suspiciously close to being in a fit of the sullens. Leander realised he was still unforgiven for his cavalier treatment of her the last time they had met. His conscience made him uneasy, for he had not meant to hurt her, yet at the same time it would not let him repair the damage. Better for her to continue with a low opinion of him than to have false hopes renewed.

He breathed a sigh of relief when Lady Annesley finally swept her prize off to display her elsewhere. Some ladies, like Lady Davenport, kept their daughters away from him, but others continued to dangle after him in the most unsubtle way. He did all that was required of him, talking, listening, dancing. By the time the hour was sufficiently advanced for him to leave without causing comment, he had lived through a thousand lifetimes.

Relieved beyond measure to escape the crowded house, Leander drew a deep breath of the night air as he strode swiftly away from the scene of his humiliation. Before he could fully relax, a voice sounded behind him. "Stay a moment, Ockley. I'll bear you company."

The linkboys had been busy along the street, and Leander easily recognised Sir John Gillingham's rotund figure hurrying after him. Leander held out his hand to the man. "I'm in your debt, Sir John," he said frankly.

Sir John's grey eyes were shrewd as he briefly took Leander's hand. "I don't wish to see your mother hurt, Ockley."

"Neither do I." Leander heard the defensiveness and guilt in his voice. He knew how his actions had opened his mother up to that possibility.

The older man hesitated before speaking again. "Tell me to go to the devil if you wish," he said at last. "But your recent behaviour is not what I have come to expect of you."

Leander took a sharp breath at the man's impertinence. He was about to make a swift put-down when he saw the expression on Sir John's face. The man's gaze conveyed both his concern for Leander and his disappointment in him. That stung Leander as none of the gossip had.

"It was a temporary lapse of judgement," he said through

clenched teeth, turning to continue on his way.

Sir John kept pace beside him in silence, allowing Leander to regain some sort of equilibrium. "There is another matter about which I wish to speak to you, Ockley," he said at last.

"Which is?" He could not hide the wariness in his tone as he glanced sideways to find Sir John's gaze on him.

"I believe you are not unaware that I admire your mother."

Leander's lips twitched. "It does not come as a complete surprise to me."

There was a softness in Sir John's voice when he replied. "I'm aware of the care with which you have discharged your duty towards her."

Leander looked at him, startled.

"I have admired her for some time," Sir John offered in explanation, before continuing. "Your care of your mother is, however, a pleasure of which I would like your permission to deprive you."

Leander stopped and offered his hand again, holding the man's gaze. "Sir John, there is no one to whom I would rather relinquish that pleasure. I hope you make her as happy as she deserves to be."

"I have every intention of so doing," Sir John agreed, taking his hand and clasping it firmly. "Thank you, Ockley."

They walked a little further before their paths diverged and Leander continued towards Green Street. At least with Sir John offering for his mother, she would be distanced from any subsequent unpleasant effects of his ill-judgement. He realised belatedly that might be why Sir John had made his declaration now. Whatever the cause, he could be nothing but pleased for her.

As for himself, his overriding emotion was one of immense gratitude to Sir John for saving him from the worst consequences of his actions. He realised now that the very select nature of the gathering had been to his disadvantage. Those with less social cachet would not have shown their judgement so openly. His title and fortune would have ensured he was not entirely unwelcome in society, but he cared desperately that, without Sir John's intervention, he would no longer have been trusted with innocents.

His only consolation was the cynical knowledge that whatever malicious tales Arden and his retinue might put about on their return to town, society would refuse to believe them. Publicly, at least. People might whisper in corners, but none would repeat the stories openly. The members of the *ton* would do anything to avoid looking foolish. To admit that Leander had duped them about the accuracy of the rumours was unthinkable. No, the answer must be that the reports of his close association with Arden were untrue.

The very thought of Arden caused Leander's chest to constrict in rage and humiliation. Every time the man caused another outrage, the catalogue of his misbehaviour would be told, including the infamous, if unproven, stories involving the Earl of Ockley. As long as the man breathed, there would be scandal attached to his name, and as long as there was scandal, speculation about Leander's moral turpitude would never be forgotten.

Well, that was no more than he deserved, he acknowledged as he climbed the steps to his front door. He had been foolish beyond belief, and now he reaped the bitter harvest of his stupidity.

As he dressed the following morning, deep anger burned steadily in Leander. It was the hypocrisy that most enraged him. He would wager a considerable part of his fortune that many of the gentlemen present last night had entered into arrangements with ladybirds, be they opera dancers, actresses, or others of dubious reputation. He would not be surprised if some of the ladies there had known congress with one not their husband. Yet they took it upon themselves to judge Arden because he did not hide his indulgences. The duke's rank ensured most doors remained reluctantly open to him, but he was unwelcome in the highest echelons.

Leander had known this when he chose to accept the man's invitations. Even so, he had not been prepared for the ferocity of the reaction he had met. Those who had called Leander friend, had wished to call him son-in-law, had meant none of it when they did so. He desired nothing less than to spend time with any of them, yet he knew he must in order to ensure no slurs attached to his name.

He found he did not care any longer for his own sake. He would happily tell all those who had been present last night to go to the devil and not give them another thought. However, he had to think of his as yet unidentified new wife and their children. Any opprobrium that attached to him would reflect on them, and he would not allow those who bore no fault to be hurt by his actions. As he thought it, he realised that his reluctance to marry again had somehow transformed into a deep aversion. He could no longer bear the prospect of a life that offered nothing more than pleasantness.

He would wait upon Arden's return and confound any lingering gossip by continuing in his usual behaviour and having no interaction with the man. He would then retire to his estate and follow his father's example by staying there. He would eventually fulfil his obligations and marry again, although the precise timing of that event remained hazy. The dowager could continue to enjoy her way of life under Sir John's aegis. Henry would continue to be Henry, alas, yet he would be abroad again soon and would once more become the problem of the French.

The thought of the peace of his country home, away from prying eyes, vicious tongues, and all artifice, almost destroyed Leander's resolve to wait. He could leave today, drive himself there directly, and have his household follow as necessary. For a few moments he indulged in the fantasy, but he knew he could not. His retreat would look to be precisely that. No, he had somehow to survive until Arden returned to town, and then his life would once more be his own.

CHAPTER SEVENTEEN

L eander bade Sir John a good afternoon as they passed on
the steps of the townhouse. It was no accident that he left
as the man arrived, for Sir John had been an almost constant
visitor since their interview two weeks previously. Leander
liked the man, but there was only so much he could take of
his mother dimpling and blushing like a girl. At least in her
pleasure at Sir John's courtship, she had forgiven Leander his
ill-judged behaviour. The *ton* too had to all outward purposes
forgiven him. The expressions in people's eyes, however, and
the conversations cut short at his approach informed him that
all was not forgotten.

As Leander entered the park on his chestnut mare, Ramsbottom rode up to him. Leander was surprised, for he and the
viscount had never been on close terms. As always, he found
it an effort not to concentrate on the growth that adorned the
man's nose but to look at his eyes. When he did, he discovered
that Ramsbottom's stare held both triumph and the hint of a
challenge.

"You must wish me happy, Ockley," the viscount declared.
"Miss Westcourt has done me the honour of accepting my offer."

So that was it. Leander was not surprised. For the past two
weeks, he had accompanied his mama to those functions she
had expressed a desire to attend, yet he had been as elusive as
manners would permit when it came to dancing with young
ladies, including Miss Westcourt. His character was now tar-
nished. It would take only an unquiet tongue to cast

aspersions upon the reputation of any young lady to whom he appeared to show favour. It had become increasingly obvious that, rather than pursue what appeared to be a forlorn hope, Lady Annesley would settle for a match that was less glittering, if still highly respectable.

Leander responded suitably to Ramsbottom. The challenge in the viscount disappeared as he realised Leander was no competitor of his, and he retired to Lady Annesley's barouche, pulled up beneath a horse chestnut tree. Leander watched for an instant, saw the pink-cheeked pleasure that was Miss Westcourt's at the eager attentions of her swain, and turned away. That was a conclusion he was pleased to see. Why it left him feeling somehow empty, he could not explain.

Leander rode on, returning acquaintances' greetings from a distance to avoid being drawn into conversation. He was glad to see Jack Sittingbourne promenading with his wife. Jack continued to invite him to spar at Gentleman Jackson's and had said nothing of any rumours. While they were no longer as close as they had been at Oxford, he was one whom Leander counted a true friend.

He nodded stiffly in return to Percy Stanford, whose unanswered invitations had reached embarrassing proportions since the night two weeks ago, but did not check his horse's stride. Instead, he pushed his mare on, wishing for nothing more than an invigorating ride over open country, taking whatever obstacles were in their way. Soon, he reminded himself. It would not be long before he could retire to the country and please himself.

His agreeable reflections stuttered to a halt. Someone was on the ride ahead of him, coming towards him. The exquisitely fitted coat of blue superfine, the white buckskins, and the polished top boots could belong to any number of gentlemen, but there could be no mistaking the muscled perfection of the figure, let alone by one so intimately familiar with every inch of it.

Leander's mare fretted under his rigid hand as his breath came unevenly. He could not turn away and pretend not to have seen him, for he was already too close for that to be credible. Any onlookers would deduce that Leander was deliberately avoiding Arden, and that would cause further speculation. Furthermore, he refused to give the man the satisfaction of seeing him turn tail.

Leander was therefore first to speak as the horses approached one another.

"Arden." It didn't sound like his voice, but he was pleased to hear how steady it was. His gaze was fixed firmly between his horse's ears, but at the last moment he could not prevent himself from glancing sideways to catch a glimpse of Arden's face.

Arden's eyes were concentrated on him. They gleamed as they met his gaze. "Leander," he welcomed, swinging his horse around to accompany him.

Leander was breathless for an instant at the man's temerity, then fury burned inside him. "I did not invite your company."

Something flickered in Arden's face before his lips curved into that familiar, hated, mocking smile.

"Leander, I am hurt," he protested. "Such coolness towards me." He glanced down and, without thinking, Leander followed his gaze to find Arden's hand caressing the handle of his whip. "Did you not enjoy our last ride together?"

The surge of rage blinded him, deafened him, for an instant perhaps, or an eternity. When it receded, Leander was deadly calm.

"You have had what you wanted from me." He held Arden's taunting eyes steadily. "There is nothing further to be said."

With that, he wheeled his mare round and rode away,

careless of any possible watchers.

"My lord?" Pickett's voice penetrated. Leander was vaguely aware that he had been speaking for some time. "My lord, are you unwell?"

His butler's concerned face came into focus. He became aware that he was standing in the book room and that his hand throbbed dully. Glancing at it, he saw blood dripping. He looked at Pickett, not understanding.

"It was the bookcase, my lord." Pickett was carefully matter of fact.

Dim memories of rage, of hitting out, the satisfaction of things breaking and smashing.

"May I see to your lordship's hand?" Pickett was talking gently and calmly to him as though he were a fractious colt, liable to lash out at the least provocation. Damn it all, as if it wasn't enough for him to make a hideous mull of everything in his life, he had now convinced the faithful family retainer of his madness.

With an effort, he regained his composure. "I'm perfectly well, Pickett. Please bring me some brandy."

"Yes, my lord." The butler looked searchingly at him for a moment before retreating.

Leander stared unseeingly at the broken pane of glass in the bookcase beside him. For an instant, he could have sworn that Arden had been pleased to see him, yet the man had gone on to mock him with that reference to the whip. His cheeks burned as he tried to deny the memories that came flooding back. Arden had been using him, and he had let it happen, doing anything and everything the man had wanted. Worse still, he had made no secret of his enjoyment of doing so, or of his delight in Arden's company.

He looked up sharply as Pickett came back into the room. His lips lifted as he saw the truly estimable man brought not only brandy but a length of soft cloth. Thanking him, Leander wrapped it around his hand.

"May I be of further assistance, my lord?"

Without looking up, Leander shook his head. The door closed softly behind the butler, leaving Leander to survey the redness that began to soak through the white cloth. He found himself reminded of the time they had fenced, when Arden's blade had drawn blood. His eyes closed in denial of the memories that followed of Arden kneeling beside him, his warm breath on Leander's skin . . .

Hell and the devil take it, he was not going to let Arden triumph. If ever he saw the man again, he would be as composed as Arden himself.

Leander rode in the park the following day, his heart beating fast as he searched among the riders for the familiar arrogant figure. He was determined to conduct himself in the most unexceptionable manner should they encounter one another. Arden needed to know that Leander cared nothing for all that had happened between them. But his determinations were in vain, for he saw no sign of Arden.

Returning home after many tedious conversations with those also taking advantage of the fashionable hour, Leander found his mother in the drawing room with Henry and Burnage. They were hunting through a pile of cards and letters. The dowager was increasingly distracted by the thought of Henry's departure, and her search for invitations to events to which her youngest son could accompany her had grown relentless. Judging from Henry's resigned expression, she would not be refused.

Leander felt none of the sympathy for his brother's predicament that might be expected. Since their last conversation, Leander had gone to some lengths to avoid Henry due to the air of generous condescension that now suffused him. Henry appeared to have forgiven him for his transgression, and his air of patient forbearance left no doubt that he believed Leander to have learned from his foolish mistake.

Leander joined the domestic party at his mother's insistence, managing to ignore the constant commentary as she picked through the pile. Until, that was, she exclaimed at a mysterious letter addressed to the earl. He rose to his feet and took it from her, frowning as he saw the direction. The hand was familiar, but he could not immediately place it.

Returning a platitude to his mother's questions about the sender, he regained his seat, where he was able to open the billet in comparative privacy. He found himself informed that Mrs Howarth would be pleased to receive him if he cared to call that afternoon. Leander screwed up the note, cursing under his breath. Thoughts of Caroline had not crossed his mind once since his return to London. She deserved better treatment than that.

It appeared that Caroline agreed with him. As soon as he arrived, he understood the purpose of this interview. It was to be a polite termination of their arrangement. He was relieved, having spent the past hour wondering how he might effect the same himself without hurt to her. He was still fond of her, yet he could no longer continue as they had been.

What vexed him was that she gave no reason for her decision. She treated him the same as ever she had, her concern for him evident when she noticed the healing cuts on his hand and asked if he had been hurt. Her calm friendliness and fondness towards him made him believe that her decision had nothing to do with the rumours. Her dismissal smarted therefore, especially following so close upon the heels of his understanding of Arden's reasons for taking him to his bed.

When he rose from his seat and bade her farewell, she hesitated for a moment before asking in a most offhand way if he had enjoyed the Duke of Arden's house party. There was an odd tone in her voice as she mentioned Arden, which informed him as clearly as her question that she knew of the rumours. He looked away as he provided a meaningless answer.

"He is a man of resource, the duke, is he not? One who, moreover, displays a definite singleness of purpose."

"He is certainly unique," Leander agreed stiffly, highly uncomfortable at talking of the man with Caroline.

"But you must now take your leave?" she anticipated, her eyes betraying amusement at his discomfiture.

He found himself smiling back at her. He would miss her, as much for her quickness of mind and her conversation as for anything else they had shared.

With a mixture of sadness and relief, Leander kissed her cheek farewell and left.

Chapter Eighteen

The dowager was devastated and did not care who knew it. "But Henry, you *know* that I have been looking forward to this for an *age!*"

"My apologies, Mama, but I cannot refuse a senior officer's invitation." Besides which, Leander thought, the quality of Colonel Kempsford's cellar was well known and Burnage too was invited. Henry softened the blow with a dazzling smile. "I am sure my brother will be pleased to accompany you in my stead."

"Of course, Mama," Leander agreed automatically.

"But Henry has reserved a box and was to spend the whole evening with me, and now it is all spoiled."

Leander managed to maintain his smile. "I'm sure you will contrive to have a tolerable evening."

"Oh, very well," she allowed pettishly. "Although Sir John is not able to be present either."

A tactful move on Sir John's part, Leander had deduced, allowing the dowager time alone with her younger son before he returned to duty.

"You know I would wish nothing more than to accompany you, Mama," Henry assured her as he rose to his feet. "Let us hope that Kempsford may be trampled by a runaway horse before tonight."

The dowager's laughter pealed out in response to Henry's grin. "Odious boy!" she reprimanded, her good humour on its way to being restored. "Well, there is always tomorrow night, I suppose."

By the time Leander and his mother reached their box at Vauxhall Gardens, no one would have suspected that she had suffered such a calamitous blow a few short hours before. Everywhere she looked, there was another of her friends or someone about whom she had heard the most *scandalous* news. She was lit up with enjoyment as Leander seated her in their booth. Situated close to the centre of the gardens, it provided an unrivalled opportunity to survey all who passed by.

Leander arranged his features into their usual calm politeness and spent his time calculating how long it would be before he could reasonably retire to Ockley. Henry and Burnage would leave in another week. Glancing at his mother, he thought it would be easy to persuade her to a change of scene after their departure if she were as downcast as he suspected would be the case. Should she prefer to stay in town for the remainder of the Season, he would, of course, place the house and servants at her disposal.

Even his musings were eventually no longer enough to block out his mother's explanations to every passing acquaintance about why dear Henry was not with her tonight, how duty bade him dine with the colonel, and how much she would miss him when he went back to face the dangerous French. "And dear Thomas too," she would add. "He is such a comfort to Henry, to have a friend like that in the trials he faces. I do believe they are closer even than brothers."

Her effusive monologue no longer had the power to unsettle Leander — it was nothing he was not used to — but the frequency of the recitation set his teeth on edge. Seeing that she was comfortably enjoying Lady Kempe's sympathy, Leander excused himself to walk through the gardens. The summer night was alight with gaily coloured lanterns strung along the walkways, their light splashing over the walls of the Grecian temple at the end of the Long Walk, but Leander was an unappreciative audience as he wandered.

His passage disturbed an intently whispering couple on a secluded seat. He realised he was in Lovers' Walk, intruding upon those who might reasonably expect to enjoy the gardens in peace. He remembered bringing Bella here shortly after they were married and her horror when, unable to resist touching her any longer, he had swept her into the shelter of one of the small summer houses scattered around the gardens. When he had tried to kiss her, she had slapped him, her sensibilities outraged.

That had been their first quarrel. She might welcome him to her bed, but marital relations were to be kept strictly within the bedchamber. She had considered him shameless and dissolute for thinking otherwise. His lips twisted as he reflected that she had been right in her reading of his character. He had not cared that Arden took him wherever they might be — on the mahogany desk in the library, ink spilling under the onslaught to stain Leander's skin, or the chaise longue in the morning room, until Leander's seed garlanded the green silk seat, or even that first time, on the grass in the rain. Leander closed his eyes for an instant before he regained his self-control.

Turning on his heel, he strode away from the memories, back towards the centre of the gardens. Perhaps he could persuade his mother to attend the concert to be held in the pavilion later this evening, where his thoughts could be concentrated upon the music instead of wandering in so destructive a fashion. He held no great hope of this, for to sit in silence was not an activity much to the dowager's liking.

Deftly navigating the many promenading groups without stopping to converse, Leander returned to their booth. Lady Kempe had evidently moved on, and the dowager was engaged in close colloquy with yet another passer-by. His heart stopped as he recognised the figure leaning familiarly over the front of the booth to speak to her.

The dowager's tinkling laugh rang out, and when she saw Leander approaching, her eyes brightened still further and she crowed with delight. "Oh, Leander, you didn't tell me how droll your friend is. I declare, he is greatly maligned. Such pleasant company! He has been keeping me entertained while you have been gone."

Leander had scarcely taken his eyes from Arden. At length, the man turned and met his gaze, dark eyes unreadable.

"A word with you, Arden," Leander snapped out.

Arden inclined his head. "For you, Leander, anything." He returned his attention to the dowager and lifted her hand to his lips. "I look forward to resuming our conversation," he promised.

She smiled at him. Biting back a curse, Leander turned and walked off, aware through his fury that Arden was following him, the laziness of his stride somehow an insult. Stopping in one of the secluded dark walks, Leander spun round to face Arden. The lanterns' light scarcely penetrated through the trees, and the moonlight revealed little of Arden's face.

"Why have I never made your mother's acquaintance before?" he asked. "She is a delightful lady."

"Keep away from her." It was a furious snarl. "I don't know what game you think you're playing, but I will not have you bothering my mother, understand me?"

"You would rather I bothered you, perhaps?" The invitation in the velvet voice was unmistakable as Arden moved forward.

Leander took a sharp step back. "Stay away from my mother," he warned, hearing suddenly how ridiculous he sounded.

He wasn't the only one to see the absurdity of the situation. Arden laughed. "Any moment now, you'll be demanding to know whether my intentions are honourable."

"No need for that," Leander bit out. "I know they will be only dishonourable."

"You didn't mind that once, Leander," Arden's voice was low. "Why so proper now?"

Even in the gloom, he saw Arden's expression change, yet he was unprepared when Arden moved swiftly forward and pulled Leander to him. Arden's mouth descended on his, persuading his lips to open and admit his seeking tongue. Leander gasped at the response that rocked his body, focusing in his cock. Drowning in the kiss, he clutched at Arden, holding him close as the comfort of that well-loved body against his swamped his defences. His mind, his body, his whole being was consumed by Arden. A sound of need resonated deep in his throat, echoed by Arden as he pulled Leander tight against him.

For one heady moment, Leander opened himself fully to Arden. This was all he wanted, all that mattered. Then the nagging knowledge at the back of his mind became reality. This was precisely what Arden wanted, to overwhelm him with physical intimacy until he could no longer think. With an incoherent protest, Leander thrust Arden away.

Arden seemed dazed as he stared at him. He moved forward, his hand reaching to Leander's face. "Leander?"

Leander stepped abruptly backwards. Allowing Arden to touch him would be his undoing.

"Do you think me so stupid?" His voice was low, but bitterness lent it strength. "Do you think I would fall for your stratagems a second time, allow you to parade me like a lapdog before the *ton* for your amusement and their disgust?" His lip curled. "You may save yourself the effort, Arden. My turpitude is already the talk of London. I should congratulate you, I suppose, on achieving your aim."

Arden stood as though rooted to the spot. "That was not my intent," he began at last.

"So you had no intention of sullying my reputation and that of my family?" Leander's voice lashed the night air. "Why else would you do what you did?"

Arden was silent, his lips twisting under Leander's furious glare.

"I have already told you, I wish for nothing more to do with you." Leander's tone was satisfyingly cool and unemotional. "Do not trouble my family again. They are nothing to do with whatever aberration of judgement may have been mine. I wish you good day." He executed a sketchy bow and strode away, slightly unnerved by Arden's continuing silence.

He turned blindly into another of the secluded paths, away from everyone. The man had no more purchase on him. He thrust aside the memory of that kiss. Whatever it was the man did that spoke to his baser part, he would not admit it. He would not permit the memories to surface. All that mattered was that he had seen that arrogant, manipulative character at a loss for words and that it was he, for once, who had the ordering of their encounter. Better still, it was over. The whole disastrous chapter was finished, never to be revisited.

He finally found his way back to their booth. A frown spoiled the beauty of the dowager's face when she saw Leander entering the box. Lady Beaumont and Lady Linton, seated beside her, looked at the identical expressions on mother and son's faces and swiftly excused themselves, leaving the booth in a rustling of silk dresses.

"Why did you whisk the duke away?" the dowager demanded. "We were having such fun until you spoiled it all. Your brother would never have done such an ill-mannered thing, you know."

"What did Arden say to you?"

"You're so abrupt sometimes, Leander," she rebuked him. "The duke was kind enough to enquire after my health. He seemed to have been under the impression that I had been ill, although he realised as soon as he saw me that nothing could have been further from the truth." Her frown vanished and she laughed delightedly at the recollection as she smoothed an imaginary crease in her skirt. "I told you, did I not, that this gown suited me?"

"*Mama.*" Leander was frustrated beyond belief. "You yourself warned me from him, and here you are, publicly talking to him!"

"Well, yes, possibly I did say something of the sort," allowed his mother. "Yet that was before I met him. Such a charming man! I know he has a rakish reputation, yet handsome young men will be a little wild, you know. I daresay dear Henry has broken more than a few hearts. He does look so *dashing* in his regimentals. But now that I have met the duke, I am sure his reputation is mostly undeserved."

His eyes closing in defeat, Leander settled himself again next to his mother. Damnation, but he'd be glad to pass the task to Sir John of protecting her from herself. At least there was one thing of which he could now be sure, and that was that Arden would not trouble her, or him, again.

CHAPTER NINETEEN

Leander woke suddenly, his heart pounding. It had been a dream, that was all. Yet it had seemed so real — he and Arden in the gardens, their kiss holding and deepening while their hands searched frantically, tearing open clothing until finally they were pressed skin to warm skin. Leander's cock had been hard and desperate as he felt the full hot flesh pushing eagerly against his. He had moaned into Arden's mouth, rubbing himself frantically against Arden's cock until he whimpered and his seed spattered Arden's skin.

Arden had finally released his mouth, allowing him to slide down until he was on his knees, eagerly taking Arden's cock into his mouth. He used every refinement of the skill that he had learned from Arden, intent only on Arden's pleasure, until Arden groaned as he shuddered and came in Leander's mouth. Afterwards, Leander had rested his head against Arden's hip, one hand lightly tracing a muscular thigh through the soft leather of his breeches.

"I love you, Arden," he had whispered.

Leander's eyes closed as he tried to dispel the recollection of Arden's mocking laughter at his declaration. Turning over, he encountered damp evidence that his release had not been only in his dream. He moved sharply to the other side of the bed and hauled the covers up over himself, desperate to forget.

Later that day, Leander returned from his customary ride in the park and found Henry alone in the drawing room. The

145

scattered pile of cards and invitations beside him on the sofa indicated that the dowager had enlisted his help in identifying entertainments at which he might spend his last few evenings of leave. It had become their daily ritual and was one with which Leander found no fault as it meant that he didn't have to sort through a mound of papers to find the bills.

Henry surged to his feet at his brother's entrance, his hand tightening to crush the billet in his hand as he glared at Leander. "Devil take it, Lea," he accused furiously. "What madness has seized you?"

Leander paused, wondering what it was that his brother referred to now.

"You may care nothing for your own name, but to introduce a man of such reputation to Mama goes beyond anything!"

Guilt made Leander defensive. "I did not introduce them!" he threw back. "God above, Henry, do you think I would do such a thing?"

"Frankly, Lea," he confessed, an edge to his voice, "I no longer have a notion what you will do next, only that the consequences will be damned unpleasant for your family."

Leander's teeth were gritted. "Arden will not bother Mama again. I have made sure of that."

He turned to leave, not wishing to spend an instant longer in his brother's judgemental presence.

Henry snorted. "If not for you, she would not have been subjected to his attentions to begin with."

Leander swung back on his brother. "Stow it. He did not go beyond the line with her, as well you know. It would have been peculiar behaviour in her indeed to cut one of her son's acquaintances, and it will not happen again. You have said more than enough on this matter."

Henry stepped forward, shoulders squared. "It seems to me I have not said enough. Damn it, you told me that you would have nothing more to do with him, yet not only do you arrange this assignation but you drag Mama into it."

His jaw dropping, Leander stared at his brother. "I suggest you return to whichever asylum is currently missing a lunatic," he said at last. "Last night's meeting was coincidence, no more."

A harsh laugh escaped Henry. "Why would he approach Mama if not to speak to you? Do you think me a half-wit?"

"As it happens, Henry, I do."

Henry's brow darkened still further. Leander turned and walked out, nodding curtly to Burnage as they passed on the landing. The worst of it was that Henry had been justified in his anger. Were it not for Leander's friendship with Arden, his mama would never have been placed in such a position. The galling knowledge that he had given Henry something else with which he might legitimately reproach his older brother did not help to reanimate any feelings of fraternal amity within Leander's breast.

He scarcely saw Henry over the next few days, for both he and Burnage were engaged elsewhere. Leander welcomed the fact until, one evening, he found himself dining alone. His mama and Henry and Burnage were all absent, though he had lost sight of which event it was that enjoyed their presence.

He sat at the dining table long after the covers had been cleared, steadily making his way through the port. He was reluctant to move, for to move would mean yet another empty room, where there was nothing to do and no one to talk to. The possibility of going out for the evening had fleetingly occurred to him but had been as swiftly discarded. He no longer wished to pass his time in the company of those who had, however briefly, revealed to him their true colours, and he suspected that Jack would be happily engaged with Mrs Sittingbourne. During their most recent meeting, Jack had confided to Leander that Mrs Sittingbourne had not known quite how to go on as a married lady and had avoided Jack's presence so that he might not realise this. Leander was not sure he understood what the problem had been, but he did comprehend the new happiness in Jack's face.

Sitting in the brightly lit room, the abundance of candles somehow emphasising its emptiness, he tried not to think of Jack and Mrs Sittingbourne dining together. Or to compare this with the dinners at Arden's country house, where the company had been relaxed and the after-dinner conversation riotous. Those times when he had stayed, that was. There were several occasions when he and Arden had left early to be by themselves.

Damnation, why had he allowed himself to remember? He ignored the beginnings of desire, as he had since returning to London, and poured himself another glass of port. He was vaguely surprised to see how far the level in the decanter had lowered as he tore his thoughts away from the memories of Arden's velvet mouth moving over his skin. Surely those long nights together must have meant something to the man.

What if they had, and Leander had hastened to a wrongful conclusion about Arden's motives, misled by Henry's dislike of him? Although, if that were the case, why had Arden not defended himself against Leander's accusations at Vauxhall? Because what he had said was true, he surmised cynically. He splashed more port into his glass, his hand unsteady. Or perhaps Leander's wild allegations had angered Arden beyond the ability to find words. For the first time, he regretted that the darkness of their encounter had prevented him from seeing the man's face clearly. He closed his eyes briefly as he considered the dreadful possibility that he had wronged Arden.

Yet whatever Arden's motives had been in seeking him at Vauxhall, they did not change the fact of his behaviour when Leander had been called home by Henry. There he hesitated.

Arden knew now that the dowager had not been unwell. If nothing else, Leander owed the man an apology for Henry's clumsy subterfuge. He turned the glass slowly in his hand, watching the way the tawny liquid reflected the candlelight. He needed Arden to know he had not been party to his brother's deceit. Draining the remains of the port, he rose determinedly to his feet.

Leander took a hackney to Arden's residence. He would not call for his carriage and have the entire household know of his destination, and when he began to walk, he found that his gait was not entirely steady. He stumbled out at the end of his journey and made his way determinedly up the steps to Arden's townhouse. The door opened before he had finished beating the knocker in an uneven tattoo.

He pushed past the footman. "Where is he?"

The man scrambled backwards to block his way. "His Grace is not receiving visitors, sir."

Leander's head cocked. He had heard a familiar voice. "The devil he isn't," he returned. He strode towards the door from where the sound had come, only to find himself impeded by the damned footman. The man was pleading breathlessly with Leander as he attempted to stop his forward momentum without committing the cardinal sin of grappling with a member of the Quality.

Leander refused to be diverted. He was vaguely aware of the man disappearing down the hallway and calling for Mr Ferndean to come immediately, but he could not care for that because he had heard Arden. He pushed open the door, revealing a small parlour and Arden seated before the fireplace.

Rupert Ogborne was kneeling between his open legs. Arden's hands were wrapped relentlessly in Ogborne's blond hair, pushing the man's mouth down on his cock. Leander watched Arden's head fall against the back of the chair, his eyes lidding as Ogborne moved, taking him deeper and faster until Arden was groaning, just as he had groaned for Leander.

He must have made some sound, for Arden's gaze flicked suddenly to where he stood motionless in the doorway. Leander turned away, pulling the door sharply closed behind him, and stumbled to the front door. He somehow found himself out of the square, out of sight of the house, and clutching convulsively at cold metal railings as he tried to deny what he had seen — Arden's loose-limbed sprawl as he surrendered to his enjoyment, before his eyes met Leander's gaze. There had been the briefest instant of shock on his face, swiftly overlain by a smile full of satisfaction at Leander's inability to stay away from him. *God.* Leander could not bear to remember the expression on his face.

He pushed frantically through the crowded streets in a way that made him no friends. He was desperate to keep walking so that he might not remember, might not think of the utter depth of humiliation that was his. He hated Arden viscerally, but he hated himself even more.

When he returned to his senses sometime later, he realised he had no idea where he was. Impulsively, he hailed a passing hackney and demanded to be taken to the nearest drinking shop. The jarvey at first demurred, judging Leander to be out of his way in this part of London, but a few choice phrases persuaded him otherwise. He left Leander outside an alehouse in Tothill Fields. The area was a haunt of some of the more adventurous young bloods who patronised insalubrious establishments in a search for excitement sadly lacking in the staid parties of the *ton*.

Leander had never before been anywhere like this, but he barely noticed the grim exterior of the place. Entering, he checked for an instant as the smoke from clay pipes caught his throat and stung his eyes. This did not deter him, and he demanded whatever was their strongest drink.

Some considerable time passed before anything disturbed

Leander in his aim of drinking himself unconscious. He had set himself with gusto to the task of forgetting his reasons for being here. Forgetting, indeed, most everything. He had not once considered how he might find his way home again from wherever here might be.

"Ockley! What the devil are you doing here?"

He looked up from his fierce concentration on his drink to find Asbury standing there, looking decidedly odd. Pleased to see a friend, he blinked, trying to work out what was different about the man before his brain gave up the unequal struggle.

"Drinking," he explained, taking an illustrative gulp before pushing his beaker in Asbury's general direction. "Like some? S'good."

Asbury picked it up and sniffed, recoiling suddenly. "God, man, that'll send you blind if you're not accustomed to it."

"Am accustomed," Leander responded smugly. "Been drinking it f'r hours. Blue Ruin, tha's it."

Asbury was wrestling him to his feet. "If that's Blue Ruin, I'm a parson's aunt. Bad brandy, that's what that is. Come on, I'm getting you out of here. How in hell did you come to be here anyway?"

"Hackney," Leander helpfully supplied.

He didn't resist as Asbury moved him towards the door and out into the street, although he did offer the observation, "Only jus' 'rived—can't wanna leave."

"I'm getting you out of here. Look at you, man. It's a wonder you haven't had your throat slit for that diamond pin in your cravat."

Leander looked down at himself before turning his gaze back on Asbury. He was dressed anonymously, with a kerchief rather than a cravat around his neck and boots lacking their usual high polish. That's what was different about him, he realised. "Look better'n you."

"Yes, and that's the problem. Who in God's name pointed you to such a place on your own?"

He was pulling Leander onwards, regardless of the difficulty Leander had negotiating the cobblestones underfoot.

"Don't need pointing," Leander informed him pugnaciously. "Do what I want."

"Yes, and don't we know it. God, I don't recall when I last saw Arden in such a taking as when you left. He was not best pleased."

Leander knew a stab of satisfaction. "Spoiled his game."

"I don't know about that," Asbury returned. "You certainly spoiled his temper. We were all ready to return to town long before he was."

Leander had pursued his own train of thought. "Bastard."

"You'll thank me in the morning," his companion assured him. "Come on, I'm finding you a hackney and sending you home."

"Not you. Him. Bastard's fucking Ogborne. Saw 'em."

"Is he?" Asbury responded without interest. "Well, he's not been precisely discriminating these past two weeks, so I can't say it's a surprise." He let go of Leander long enough to signal to a hackney, grabbing him once more as he lurched disastrously. Ignoring the jarvey's protest that the gentleman looked as though he were about to cast up his accounts, he helped Leander into the carriage.

"There you go, Ockley," he said, assisting the unsteady earl to sit upright. "I hope to God you remember where you live because I have no idea, and I have to go back to meet Broughton."

Leander blinked up at him. "Like you, Asbury, even if y'are interfering nuisance."

Asbury stood looking at Leander for a moment. "Oddly enough, Ockley, I return your regard. Call on me when you're recovered — if you remember a word of this conversation, that is."

He closed the door and instructed the driver to take his passenger towards a more godly area of the capital.

Leander remembered nothing of getting out of the hackney, just that the world was spinning around him and he was bending over. A burning stream ran through his throat and mouth as his stomach voided itself, sourly wrenching even when there was nothing more to follow. Finally, it stopped. Wiping his mouth on his sleeve, Leander staggered on, the surface under his feet damnably uneven, until paving stones were suddenly cool beneath his cheek. He was reluctant to move. To do so would be to cause everything to start spinning again. No, better to lie here and sleep.

Voices, someone shaking him. "Ockley, for God's sake, man."

Blurred faces were looking down at him. He was being pulled up, his arms put around people's necks as he tried to support his own weight with his legs, but they would not work properly. He remembered nothing further.

Chapter Twenty

L eander awoke the next morning in a bedchamber he didn't
recognise, his head pounding and his insides stirring un-
easily. A bowl was placed beside him on the bed, and he
leaned over an instant before his stomach expelled its meagre
contents. He lay back shivering, his arm flung across his eyes.

Some time later, after his stomach had rebelled again, he
heard curtains being drawn and a familiar voice. "Drink this."

He cracked open his eyes against the painful light and saw
Sir John Gillingham thrusting a glass at him. Carefully propping himself up, he waited for the expected wave of nausea.
Relieved when it didn't come, he clumsily reached for the
glass of small beer. He drank it all and handed the empty
glass back to Sir John, slowly letting himself back down
against the pillows.

The man put it to one side and stood looking at him, his
arms crossed disapprovingly. "Tell me, Ockley, have I been
deceived in your character all these years?" His eyes betrayed
his distaste as he looked at Leander. "I thought you the epit-
ome of responsibility, yet first you participate in one of Arden's notoriously disgraceful gatherings, and then Lionel and
I find you rolling in the gutter, drunker than a brewer's cat.
Certainly in too reprehensible a condition to be taken to your
home where your mother would hear of it." He shook his
head. "God knows we all dip too deep sometimes, but most
of us don't drink ourselves to oblivion. How came you to be
in such a state?"

Leander's eyes closed. He could not remember how he had

come to be here, only the reason for it, which he wished he could forget. And he was in no condition to cope with sermons. God, his head hurt.

"Is this behaviour I am to expect regularly from my son-in-law?" Sir John pursued mercilessly.

He turned his head away. "No."

There was a pause, and then the bed dipped and creaked as Sir John sat down. "I thought I was not wrong in my reading of you. And you seemed to find no pleasure in such dissipation last night. Mind telling me why you did it?"

The sympathy in his voice was too much for Leander in his weakened condition. He shook his head, keeping his face averted.

"Very well." Sir John hesitated slightly. "If I can be of help, Ockley, let me know."

He quietly left the room, leaving Leander to his humiliating reflections. He did not deserve the man's sympathy. The stupidity of his port-driven imaginings left him mortified. How could he have been feeble-minded enough to believe that Arden had not been using him? God, the thought of calling upon Arden like some moon-struck idiot was enough to make his stomach turn even without the brandy. Compared to that humiliation, the possibility of his drunken stupor being witnessed by members of the *ton* paled into insignificance. After all, it was no more than they had come to expect from him. At least it might keep some of the matchmaking mamas from his back for a while.

He lay there until he was driven from the bed by the foul taste in his mouth, needing to rinse it away. He was too ashamed to hold his bloodshot gaze in the looking glass for long. Instead, he ran his fingers through his hair in an approximation of combing, drew on over the ruins of the previous night's clothes the dressing gown that Sir John's man had left for him, and ventured out to where Sir John was taking breakfast.

Leander declined all sustenance except a cup of coffee. Sir John was busy buttering the rolls on his plate, which provided Leander with an opportunity to watch the man unobserved. He had always believed him to be a good man, but this level of kindness was unanticipated.

"I miss my wife," Leander said. He hadn't known he was going to say it until the words were out. Sir John laid down his knife and looked at him. "Arden was a distraction," he added, for there had been sympathy in Sir John's face, and Leander did not deserve it—he needed to remind Sir John of his culpability. Although missing Bella was the root of his behaviour, it was not the reason for it. Her absence no longer crippled him, but he had found himself unable to remember how to live fully without her. Arden's company had been exciting, exhilarating, overwhelming—he had appealed to all of Leander's senses and overcome them until he had been lost, knowing only that he was *alive.*

Sir John nodded, although Leander was reasonably certain he did not understand. "I have sometimes thought the Duke of Arden not to be as far beyond salvation as he has been painted," he said, surprisingly. "I believe it is in part a case of the sins of the father being visited upon the son."

"His father?"

"He was at least as vice-ridden as his son, but his defining trait was cruelty. To women, to his servants, to his horses. And to his wife."

Leander took another sip of his coffee, trying to clear the cloudiness in his head as Sir John settled deeper in his seat, pleasurably preparing to recount the private business of another. For the first time, Leander saw how well-suited he was to the dowager. He had visions of them spending long, happy evenings together, exchanging the latest *on-dits.*

"His young wife eloped with a dancing master when the

present duke was five years old," Sir John said. "They fled overseas, for Arden's rage was terrible. But the dancing master died from the plague and the duchess was left alone, penniless, in Venice. Some of her friends tried to help her, but Arden would not. He divorced her, forbade all mention of her name, and took care to spend the money she had brought to the marriage on Cyprians and shameful spectacle. It's said he hated his son, for he reminded him of her." His face was briefly sober, as if recognising that real people and tragedies lay behind even the most scandalous gossip. "When he died nine years later, no one mourned him, not even a dog."

Or his son? But Leander did not ask the question, for he did not wish to know the answer. "What happened to the duchess?" he asked instead.

"Died in destitution two years after the dancing master. So you see that the present duke was mired in scandal not of his making before he was out of petticoats." Sir John's eyes crinkled at the corners, as if he realised the ridiculousness of what he said. "I do not mean to imply the man is blameless for he behaves atrociously, but the gossips who so enjoy their horror at his misdeeds perhaps forget the circumstances of his early life."

Sir John turned his attention back to his meal, leaving Leander to consider this new information. He remembered the size of Arden's country house and thought of a small boy growing up there, alone except for an army of servants and a father with a reputation for viciousness.

He caught himself and redirected his thoughts. Regardless of the duke's history, he never wanted to see the man again.

Leander returned to Green Street late in the afternoon. Pickett, appearing not to notice his pale and unshaven state, informed him that a visitor had called for him once that morning and twice that afternoon. He had appeared most desirous of speaking to Leander. Leander took the card that had been left and swayed slightly when he saw Arden's name on it. He thanked Pickett automatically before instructing him that he was not at home to visitors and retiring to his room to wash and change.

Once there, he took great care over shredding the card into as many small pieces as he could manage, desperately wishing he could do the same to himself. After the previous night, Arden must believe that he still exercised the same power over Leander as he once had and intended to put that to use again. Either that, or the man wished to gloat. With a groan, Leander bent forward over the bowl and emptied the jug of water over his still-aching head. God, what a damned fool he'd been. He flicked back his wet hair, the resulting rivulets of water cold on his back as his course of action became clear.

Despite the reluctance evinced by his stomach at the thought, Leander joined his family for dinner. His mind was made up, and he wished to waste no time in informing his mother of his decision.

"I am sure Sir John will be delighted to accompany you, Mama, when you decide to join me," he assured the dowager. She was looking decidedly pettish at the news he had broken. "He is, of course, welcome to stay at Ockley for as long as he wishes."

"I think it a capital idea," Henry struck in. "By going ahead, Lea can make sure that all is ready to receive you and Sir John."

The dowager turned injured eyes on him at his betrayal. "But Henry, *no one* goes to the country at this time of year."

Henry smiled at her. "True, Mama, but just think — you will be starting a new fashion. And I think it a good idea to have something else to do once Thomas and I are gone. If you stayed here, you would undoubtedly be moped."

Reminded of her son's departure, the dowager sighed. "No

doubt you are right," she said in a small voice, toying with the trout on her plate as though her appetite had deserted her.

CHAPTER TWENTY-ONE

Leander finally knew a sense of contentment. He had arrived the previous afternoon to a warm welcome from his housekeeper, Mrs Thornton. His heart had eased after a night's sleep and a morning listening to the happenings in the lives of the principal figures in his household. Now, the delight of a good horse under him on a summer's afternoon on his own estate filled him with peace.

The larks singing overhead, the soft thud of the horse's hooves, the slight creak of the saddle, and the scent of summer grass were all things he associated intimately with Ockley. He smiled as he passed the climbing tree on which he and Henry had played so often, remembering when they had defended it tooth and nail from their cousins. The older one, George, had given Henry such a drubbing one day that the dowager had declared the boy must be removed from her house at once. They had not returned.

He stopped on the crest of the hill. As had been the intention of the genius who created the gardens, the long ride drew an observer's eye irresistibly to Ockley House. Designed by a disciple of Palladio, its symmetry and proportion were exquisite, while its light stone seemed to shine in the sun. This westerly prospect suited Leander better than the conventional southern one. He loved his home in every season and from every aspect, but parkland appealed to him more than formal gardens.

His horse began to fidget at the enforced inactivity, and Leander dismounted. He loosened the girth, unfastened the reins from one side of the bit to give the animal length enough to graze without troubling him, and sat, his back against the sun-warmed stone of the obelisk behind him, memorial to some long-dead earl. Settling himself more comfortably, he laid his head back against it, looking down on his home, feeling the sunshine warming him through his clothes. The drowsy humming of bees, the horse cropping the short turf, its tail whisking occasionally to keep the flies away, and his own deep breathing were the only sounds in the world.

Soft whickers brought him awake some time later and he opened his eyes to find his horse's head was up, its ears pricked enquiringly. He twisted his head round to follow the direction of the animal's concentration. A still figure sat on a dark horse, watching him.

For an instant, he thought he must still be dreaming, but the man swung off his horse, leaving it to wander, and approached him. He stopped close to Leander, one polished boot propped on the monument's base, an arm resting on his powerful thigh as he leaned forward to regard Leander.

Leander climbed slowly to his feet.

"What in hell's name are you doing here?" He was furious to hear that his voice shook with the shock of this unexpected visitation.

Arden's eyes glinted as he straightened. "Don't disturb yourself on my account, Leander, please. You cannot know what a charming picture you make, nestled against mother earth, your limbs sprawled in so artless and inviting a way, your eyes closed peacefully and your lips slightly apart as you breathe softly. Quite charmingly pastoral. All that is missing is your herd of cattle to drive and the haystalk in your mouth."

"What the devil do you want, Arden?" He refused to let the man see how off-balance he was, though his knuckles were white around his reins.

Arden's expression was watchful as his eyes dwelt reflectively on his face. "I consider that a most grudging welcome considering the length of journey that has been mine to visit you here, not to mention the means I have had to employ to ascertain the path you took on your ride this afternoon. Are you not going to profess yourself pleased to see me?"

"Understand this, Arden. I made an error of judgement once. That does not give you the right to hound me ever after." Leander glared into the intent eyes, so unreadable on his. "Move on to your next victim. You will gain nothing more from me." He was aware that his breath was coming swiftly, but he refused to be the first to look away.

"If that is how you feel, why did you visit me two nights ago?" The smooth voice for once held no mockery. In fact, it held no discernible emotion at all.

Leander hesitated for an instant. "To offer you my apologies for my brother's behaviour."

One eyebrow raised. "For which aspect of his behaviour in particular? His very existence demands apology, though I do not think you may properly be held accountable for that."

Suppressing his sudden urge to agree with Arden, Leander said stiffly, "I refer to his machinations in calling me back to London."

"I see." Dark eyes watched him, intent. "There was no other reason for your visit?"

Leander's laughter held a jeering undertone. "Having found you being so thoroughly entertained by one of your tame pets, why should you think there might be another reason?"

Arden's gaze dropped and his lips twisted. "Why indeed?"

Leander turned to his horse and tightened the animal's girth. "There is a tolerable inn not fifteen miles from here," he said offhandedly. "You have plenty of time to reach it before sunset. It lies on the road to London, so you will have a good start on your journey tomorrow morning."

Arden seized Leander's shoulder and dragged him round. His face was almost unrecognisable, filled with fury. "We finish this *now*," he snarled. "Speak plainly, Leander — why did you come to my house?"

Anger surged in Leander's breast, rising to meet Arden's temper. "To see if I had wronged you in my opinion of your character," he spat, his lip curling in disgust as he remembered the sight that had greeted him. "Evidently, I had not."

Arden released him. Leander glared at him for a moment longer, before turning back to his horse to refasten its reins.

"I had thought you were not coming." Arden's voice was low.

Leander spun round, his brow furrowed with impatient question. He wanted it over, done, to recover the sense of peace that had been his such a short while before, yet Arden's unusual hesitancy caught his attention and stayed his tongue.

Arden met Leander's gaze briefly, and Leander's eyes narrowed as he saw the man's uncharacteristic defensiveness. Then he realised that this was a ploy. One that he had not previously encountered, to be sure, but it was another of Arden's games.

"Why should you have expected me?" he asked contemptuously. "I had already made it clear I wished to have nothing more to do with you."

Anger flickered over Arden's face at Leander's tone, and when he spoke, his voice was harsh. "You did not come in answer?"

"In answer?" Leander repeated, angry and confused. "I don't understand you."

Arden made an impatient gesture. "That damned letter."

As he took in Leander's stare, his lip curled in a sneer. "No matter," he said. "I will leave you to your respectable life, Leander. I shall not bother you again."

He turned away and strode towards his horse, which was tearing hungrily at the grass, one foot through its reins.

"Arden?"

When there was no response, Leander led his horse after him.

"*Arden.*"

"What?" Arden snapped out, swinging round to face him.

Leander shrugged slightly. "I don't know what you mean. What letter?"

Arden's eyes were hard as they quartered his face suspiciously. "Do not presume too far, Ockley. Whatever maudlin thoughts I may have inadvisably committed to paper were due simply to an excess of brandy. Do not think to hear me repeat them."

"Arden, I don't know to what you refer. I have received no letter from you."

"My footman delivered a letter to you, the morning after our meeting at Vauxhall." His tone was sceptical. "Do you try to tell me you did not receive it?"

Leander shook his head, helplessly. "I have had no letter from you. What did it say?"

Arden's eyes were hard still. "It was delivered to your house. Do not try me too far, Ockley."

Confused, Leander cast his mind back. He had received nothing other than bills and endless invitations from Percy Stanford. Anything not addressed to him privately had been seized upon long before reaching him by his diversion-seeking mama and —

"*Henry.*" Fury surged through him. He knew it for the truth even while he could barely credit his brother with such outrageous behaviour. He glared at Arden, rage giving his voice a vicious edge. "Tell me, Arden, did you seal the letter with your ring?"

Arden's eyes narrowed. "Of course. What has that to do

with anything?"

Leander took a slow, deep breath and let it out equally slowly before he trusted himself to reply. "Everything, I should imagine. I believe that my brother, seeing your crest on a private billet addressed to me, felt it incumbent upon himself to interfere."

For a heartbeat Arden was silent, and then his face filled with wrath. "He has gone too far this time." He turned to his horse and wrenched its head up.

Leander grabbed his arm, forcing Arden back to face him. "Agreed," he gritted out. "But he is *my* responsibility."

Arden's eyes still blazed with rage, and Leander's grip tightened. "It is for *me* to deal with, no one else," he reiterated, his voice holding a threat that boded ill for his brother.

Arden's chest rose and fell swiftly as he glared at Leander. As Leander held his gaze, his breathing slowed, and his eyes began to lose their violence. "Very well," he conceded finally. "But if you wish for someone to act for you—"

Leander choked on sudden laughter. "I do not think it will come to that. He is, after all, my brother."

All desire to laugh left him as he looked into Arden's eyes. There was an uncertainty there that he had never seen before. Suddenly aware that he held the man by the arm, he released him. Arden turned and concentrated on his horse.

"The letter," Leander broached finally, his hand running over the velvet muzzle of his own mount. "What did it say?"

Arden's movements stilled for an instant, and then he became very busy checking the fit of the bridle.

"Arden," Leander said quietly.

Arden turned around, his mouth twisted self-deprecatingly. "As I said, jug-bitten maunderings, no more."

Leander's hand dropped from his horse's head to his side. Arden's gaze followed its path, then he looked back into Leander's face.

"I may have asked you to allow me to explain that matters between us were not as you thought," he said at last.

Leander's heartbeat was suddenly uneven, his throat dry. "Then do so."

Arden moved forward. "I would rather show you."

"No." Dropping his horse's reins, Leander stepped abruptly backwards. Arden stopped.

"Tell me," Leander said. He knew that if Arden were to touch him, the man would be able to convince him of anything he chose.

Arden's face was unreadable. "Very well, Leander." His voice was clipped and low. "You were right. To begin with, your seduction was a challenge, a game, no more. You were so upright and proper, and with you being brother to the self-righteous Henry Talbot, how could I be expected to resist the temptation?"

His head pounding at the man's brutal candour, Leander looked away. "You are honest, at least," he managed, his throat tight.

He was vaguely aware that Arden's gaze was on his face. "To begin with, I said." Arden's voice was rough. "It is different now."

Leander looked dazedly at him. Arden's eyes were steady on his as he moved forwards. He stopped when he was so close, they were all but touching.

"It is not like that now, Leander."

He shivered at the caress of the low voice, and then he was aware of nothing else as Arden leaned in and his lips met Leander's. Leander felt the soft warmth, and he opened to Arden, his eyes closing as Arden's tongue slowly pushed into his mouth and he tasted Arden again. His arms went blindly around Arden, hands clutching. Whimpering deep in his throat, he moved closer against the hard body, his tongue meeting Arden's, lightly stroking in a way that drew a sound from Arden.

"You see, Leander." Arden's voice was husky when at last they broke the kiss. "This is how it is now."

Leander remained pressed against Arden, feeling the warmth of his body through their clothes, pressed thigh to thigh, cock to swollen cock, breathing in Arden's heady scent.

Arden caressed his arse, causing Leander to arch in response, pushing himself closer. Leander was breathing fast, a sound escaping him as Arden's finger slowly traced the centre seam of his buckskins. Arden's tongue flicked his ear while his seeking hand slid down the front of his body, separating them so Arden could stroke Leander's cock through the soft leather of his breeches.

His heart was racing as he pulled away from Arden. "Not here," he said. "Someone might see us." He caught Arden's mouth in a brief kiss before he forced himself to stop. "The spinney. No one will disturb us there." No locals ventured near it even in daylight due to bloodcurdling tales of a headless countess and her equally headless hound. Leander had never believed in such things. At least, not since his fifteenth birthday.

Arden captured his mouth and kissed him in return, his tongue thrusting in a promise so explicit that it was all Leander could do not to whimper. Arden finally released his mouth and unfastened his waistcoat, slipping his hands underneath the loosened garment and unerringly finding Leander's nipples with his long fingers. He stroked them through the light shirt before running his nails hard across them, hungrily watching Leander's face as he gasped at the sensation. Then he stopped and pulled Leander's waistcoat together again.

"You are right," he confessed. "I should very much dislike to be disturbed in what I have in mind for you, Leander."

Chapter Twenty-Two

The ride to the spinney seemed to Leander to last forever. Each step of the way was filled with Arden's low voice telling Leander precisely what he was going to do to him once they reached the privacy of the trees, how he would use his mouth and hands to bring him to quivering desperation before he finally slid deep inside him.

They didn't take the time to tether their horses but dropped the reins and reached for one another. Arden's mouth and the feel of his body were almost more than Leander could bear. He fumbled as he tried to remove Arden's coat. Arden pulled away for an instant to assist Leander in his endeavours and then began to strip Leander of his clothing. Leander attempted to reciprocate, but Arden's hot mouth closed around his nipple, his teeth scraping the hard nub, and it was all he could do to remain standing as Arden's hand lightly stroked him through his buckskins.

Arden raised his head and looked into Leander's eyes as he stroked him again, causing Leander to whimper and push into his touch.

"Lie down, Leander."

The unevenness of Arden's voice excited him beyond bearing. He complied instantly, lying on his back in the sunlight that dappled through the branches above them. He stared up at Arden standing over him, eyes drawn irresistibly to where Arden's buckskins strained over excited flesh.

"Arden, *please*." His voice was ragged.

Arden was breathing quickly as he looked down at

Leander. "What do you want me to do, Leander?"

"Fuck me." It came out as a desperate demand.

Arden knelt beside Leander and, leaning forward, kissed him. "In a while," he promised when he drew back.

He removed Leander's right boot.

"Arden," Leander protested despairingly.

Arden paused and looked at him. "I want to see you first," he said. "I want to see your body waiting for me."

Leander closed his eyes in frustration as Arden removed his other boot, then his skilful fingers unfastened the buttons of Leander's fall. He could scarcely breathe in anticipation. He opened his eyes again in time to raise his head and watch Arden fold the flap down, exposing his eager cock. Arden leaned forward, his tongue swirling hotly over the head of his cock, sending Leander arching upwards in helpless delight.

He was still gasping when Arden stripped him swiftly of his buckskins and then stood again, looking down on him. Leander felt no self-consciousness as he lay there, watching Arden's gaze moving slowly over his body and lingering on his full cock. He stretched wantonly, the harsh edge of a twig under his shoulder interrupting the softness of the grass beneath him as he luxuriated in the warmth of the greenly filtered sunlight and the heat of Arden's gaze. As he saw Arden's eyes devouring him, he smiled slightly and opened his legs, drawing his right knee out and sliding it upwards on the grass, displaying himself further for Arden.

Arden was suddenly upon him, his tongue in Leander's mouth. Arden's hands were greedy on his skin, and then he pushed two fingers between Leander's eager lips. An instant later, Arden was sliding a slick finger inside him. Leander gasped and thrust down, wanting, needing, but somehow Arden knew and added a second finger, working him, stretching him, until finally Arden was satisfied. He withdrew his fingers and undid his buckskins, freeing his cock.

Leander bit hard into his lower lip, trying for control, as he watched Arden produce the familiar glass bottle from his pocket. Arden upended it to pour some of the liquid directly onto his hardness, his hand smoothing the viscous liquid until his cock was glistening. When the blunt head nudged against him, he forgot any attempt at control and groaned as Arden's cock slid deep inside him.

As Arden set up a rhythm, Leander wasn't even aware of crying out, just of a voice rising in the summer afternoon in unrestrained delight. Again and again, Arden's size and hardness pushed deep into him, until Leander's voice was lost and whimpers were all that remained. That was when Arden leaned forward to kiss him, and Leander came. And still Arden pushed into him, desperately now, sounds escaping him with each thrust, until he looked down at Leander's face and his hips pumped erratically as he gasped out his completion.

Leander held Arden close as he collapsed onto him. Arden's face remained hidden against Leander's shoulder until finally his breathing slowed, and he pressed a kiss against the warm skin before moving to lie beside him. Leander turned onto his side, his head propped on his fist to better observe Arden's face, unable to believe that he was not dreaming. In the space of one short hour, everything had changed beyond comprehension. The past weeks of misery were forgotten. All that mattered was that Arden was here with him.

"How did you find me?" he asked, curious. He had thought himself safely removed from everyone, yet it had taken Arden just one day to discover his sanctuary.

Arden shifted to make himself more comfortable before answering. "When I realised you did not intend to return my visit, I called upon you once more, on which occasion your butler graciously informed me that you were gone out of town. It did not take too wild a guess on my part to conclude that you were at your estate. Your butler was obliging enough to inform me, albeit in tones of shocked reproach, that this was in Surrey, *not* Lancashire as I had remembered it to be."

"Good God!" Leander stared at him with horrified fascination. "You thought me so beyond the pale?"

Arden laughed. "Not at all. But I could scarcely ask him where Ockley was."

"And I thought you had done your research." Leander shook his head in mock disgust.

"Only into those aspects that affected me at the time."

"Understandably," Leander allowed. He lay quietly for a moment before it dawned on him. "And Caroline affected you, did she not?" He sat up, frowning at Arden. "What caused her unexplained absences? You did not threaten her?"

"Leander," Arden protested, seemingly amused. "I would not do so to such a lady as she proved herself to be. I may have needed to apply a little pressure the first time, but upon the second occasion, she saw that nothing would deflect me from my intention and had the audacity to give me her unexpurgated opinion of my character and my behaviour towards you."

"The second occasion?" Leander became aware that his jaw was hanging open and swiftly shut it. "You mean she concluded our arrangement because you compelled her to?" And then he envisaged Caroline speaking to Arden in such a way and laughed. "Tell me, why did you not dispose of Henry at the same time?" He was teasing but abruptly remembered his brother's actions and compressed his lips, all humour fled. "I shall have to pay my brother a visit before he returns to his heroic deeds. I cannot believe even he would do such a thing."

"He and I do not see eye to eye," Arden said. "In his own twisted and thankfully inimitable way, he probably believes that he did you a favour."

"But still, to appropriate a sealed letter addressed to me goes beyond anything."

"I can only hope that he did not read it." Arden's voice was sour. "I do not enjoy the thought of Henry Talbot knowing anything of me that I do not choose him to know."

Leander looked quickly at him. "What did it say?"

Arden shrugged before responding in a carefully unconcerned manner. "An attempt to explain to you that things were not as you had thought and something of how I wished them to be." His lip curled. "I believe I even explained that I wrote to you rather than inflict my presence upon you. I wished to show that I took notice of your request not to trouble your family again. Had I known how your family would trouble me, I would not have been so compliant."

Leander laughed. "At least my mother will be pleased that I am overturning the ban upon contact."

Arden's eyebrow rose in query.

"Your shameless flirtation won her favour. You might be able to cut out Sir John with her if you were to try."

Arden shuddered artistically. "Leander," he complained. "Tell me that you have not given her my direction in Oxfordshire."

"Not yet," Leander admitted, settling down beside him once more. Tempting as it was to tease Arden with the prospect of a visit from the dowager, it did not compare to lying quietly with him beneath the canopy of the trees. Arden was pressed against his side, the larks sang overhead, and joy filled Leander's heart.

He had not intended to fall asleep, but he opened his eyes to find the shadows around them had moved, and Arden was now propped on one elbow, watching him. There was a new warmth in his steady regard, and Leander smiled sleepily at him.

Arden bent his head to kiss him gently, his hand tracing light patterns over Leander's chest. He then explored Leander's body with his lips and tongue until Leander was shivering under his ministrations. He was able only to cry out Arden's name as he swallowed Leander's cock, wetness and warmth tight around him. He raised his head, and the sight of his cock sliding between Arden's lips, the sight of Arden, ripped another cry from him and, without warning, his seed spilled into Arden's mouth.

He was aware of Arden moving, and he reached blindly for him, holding him close. As Leander's heaving breaths slowly eased, he relinquished his tight hold, and Arden again lay down beside him.

Leander explored Arden's body in turn, intent on showing him what he felt he should not say. With mouth and hands, he lavished care on him, employing everything he had learned Arden enjoyed, until Arden shuddered and came, Leander's name on his lips.

Afterwards, Leander lay on the soft summer grass, his head resting against Arden's hip, Arden's hand moving idly through his hair. Leander's breath whispered across his skin, following the path of the lazily moving sunlight and shadows. Listening to Arden's breathing, feeling the warmth of his body, Leander knew that this was where he belonged.

Chapter Twenty-Three

It was mid-morning before they set out for London on the following day. There had been a matter Leander needed to attend to before leaving Ockley again, something he did each time he visited. He chose the roses and cut each one himself. It was part of the ritual. He took them to the Temple of Apollo, where Bella had loved to sit and contemplate the gardens, particularly as the time for her confinement had grown closer.

On entering the temple, he paused before approaching the stone bench where she had always sat, trying to understand what was different. He realised suddenly — in the past, he had always known she was there, that if he had just managed to turn his head an instant sooner, he would have seen her. Now, there was nothing here save a beautifully proportioned empty building. He laid her favourite flowers on the seat and knelt beside it for a moment. These were the last flowers he would cut for her.

He paused at the entrance to the temple and looked back one last time, seeing crimson petals splashed on the white stone. They were the only living things the place contained, and he shivered at the realisation. Turning away from the cold empty stone, Leander set his face to the sun and strode down the hillside towards his home.

Even Pickett's equilibrium was shaken by the earl's sudden return to Green Street. He recovered valiantly to inform Leander that the dowager was gone out, as were Captains Talbot and Burnage.

This situation was soon remedied. Leander and Arden were ensconced comfortably in the drawing room when the door opened to reveal Henry.

"Come in, Henry," Leander invited cordially. "I believe you are already acquainted with His Grace the Duke of Arden."

Henry's forward momentum ceased. His head swivelled, his gaze fixing with disbelieving outrage on Arden. "Devil take it," he swore. "What in hell's name is *he* doing here?"

"Arden is my guest," Leander said calmly.

"*Leander.*" Henry turned wrathful eyes on him, struggling for words. "I must speak to you *immediately*," he finally ground out.

"Please do so," Leander said. "I'm interested to hear what excuse you intend to offer for your behaviour."

"*Alone.*" Henry's tone was dangerous.

Leander held his brother's gaze. "There is nothing you can have to say that cannot be said in front of Arden."

"God, he really has blinded you, hasn't he?" Henry snarled. "Very well, I will not scruple to tell you that you are being stupid beyond imagining. He"—and he jerked his head in Arden's direction, apparently unwilling to pollute his eyes by even looking at the man again—"he is nothing but a libertine, delighting only in depravity and vice." He flung the words at Leander. "God above, Lea, he has no end in mind other than to ruin you, and you will not see it. He has soiled your reputation enough already—continue this alliance and *no* one will receive you!"

Leander spared a swift glance for Arden. He sat apparently relaxed, a mocking smile on his lips as he regarded Henry, but dark rage burned in his eyes

"I do not intend to repeat myself, Henry, so please concentrate." Leander's voice was cold. "I will not allow you to insult my guest under my roof. If you cannot be civil, you may find accommodation elsewhere. What I do is my business and mine alone, as long as it does not affect Mama."

"And what *about* Mama?" Henry flung furiously. "You bring *him* under the same roof—"

"While you have not scrupled to fuck your lover under the same roof as her for the past God knows how many years," Leander accused. "You are a selfish hypocrite, totally unprincipled in the means you employ to achieve your ends. Your only objection to my action is that you will now be looked to for stud duty."

"Damn you, Lea, I refuse. You cannot make me!" Henry glared mulishly at his brother.

"That is your business," Leander returned disinterestedly. "I would not presume to comment on your decision."

"Damn you to hell, Leander." Henry's eyes were bright and his colour dangerously high. Then he whirled round on Arden. "I suppose *you* are satisfied now, aren't you?"

"I cannot deny that I find your brother extremely satisfying," Arden agreed smoothly. "Which is more than I was able to say about your little friend."

Henry lunged towards him, but Leander was out of his chair, a hand warningly to his brother's chest. "I have already told you, Henry."

Henry's eyes burned on his. "You are a damned stupid fool."

"I wish for the return of my property." Leander's voice was edged with fury. "And then, as far as I am concerned, you may go to the devil."

"Your property?" Henry's face reflected his confusion.

"I believe you have in your possession a letter addressed to me."

Henry's eyes flickered before he smiled in surly triumph. "I burned it."

The lack of shame, the lack of regret that his selfish action could have cost Leander his happiness, was too much for him. Without conscious intention, his fist connected with his brother's jaw. Taken by surprise, Henry went down like a felled ox, his head connecting solidly with the leg of the sofa.

Leander was left staring in amazement and knew an instant of glorious satisfaction. Arden slowly unfolded from his chair and joined him, standing over Henry's unmoving figure.

"Had I known what a punishing right you possess, Leander, I might have treated you with a little more circumspection."

"I didn't intend to do that," Leander confessed, flexing his hand somewhat gingerly.

"I am pleased you did, however, as otherwise I might have had to run him through to prevent him annoying me any further." He pulled Leander to him, his teasing eyes steady on Leander's. "And you know, it would not suit me to have to flee the country. Not now."

Leander could not help but smile at him before wrenching his mind back to other things. "What did you mean about Burnage? I take it he was the friend you mentioned?"

"I believe he had suffered a surfeit of your heroic brother one night," Arden said. "Whatever his reasons, he attended a party of mine and threw himself — with great enthusiasm, if memory serves — into the spirit of the occasion." He glanced past Leander at Henry's unconscious figure. "I would never let your brother know this, but there were so many present and enjoying themselves that night that I cannot even be sure that I had him."

Leander tried to hold back his laughter. "So Henry hates you for something you may not have done?"

Arden's eyes gleamed. "I'm not convinced his friend was in a suitable state to remember what had happened. I can only assume that he confessed what he thought to be the whole to

Talbot in a fit of remorse. I am certainly the devil incarnate as far as your brother is concerned."

"Literally, I believe, from what he intimated of your activities involving hellfire and sacrificial virgins."

"The tales are still told?" Arden asked, highly amused.

"You know of them, then. But how in God's name did such slander start?" Suspicion dawned, and he surveyed Arden through eyes that were suddenly narrowed.

"I am innocent," Arden protested, laughter in his face. "Of that, at least. I have as little knowledge of their origin as you. I concede I may not be entirely blameless of some embroidering upon occasion, for the circulation of such scurrilous rumours suits me. It ensures I am not plagued by those who would otherwise toad-eat me due to my rank."

Those who would do so comprised the entire *ton*, as Leander well knew. He could not fault Arden for doing such a thing—it had freed him entirely from the society of those for whom he cared not one whit. "It occurs to me that some refinement may be needed if the tales are to achieve permanence," he suggested. "I would recommend the addition of a more lurid element, such as drinking the blood of unbaptized infants."

"Far too commonplace," Arden dismissed enjoyably. "Besides which, I suspect blood would not mix well with brandy."

A groan from Henry interrupted them, and Leander reluctantly stepped back from Arden. In unspoken agreement, they left the room. Before they had progressed far along the landing, the dowager's voice reached them, warning of her approach up the stairs.

"It is such a *fortunate* coincidence that we met you and Henry as we did, although it was a shame he had to rush away so swiftly. Still, I know that Annabel was flattered by your attentions, and perhaps you might be able to put a good word in for dear Henry tonight."

She broke off with a startled cry when she looked up to see her eldest son standing at the head of the stairs. "Leander! Why are you back? Is something amiss?" And then she saw his companion. Her worry disappeared, to be replaced by a charming dimpled smile. "I declare, Duke, what a pleasant surprise."

She made her way up the remaining stairs with surprising speed and offered her hand to Arden. He promptly kissed it. With a delighted chuckle, the dowager looked round for her companions, who were just gaining the landing behind her. Sir John's gaze was moving between Arden and Leander, while Burnage's eyes were fixed on Arden in a manner that reminded Leander of a rabbit watching the approach of a fox.

"Sir John, Thomas, I am sure you know His Grace the Duke of Arden," she said.

Before either of them could do more than bow stiffly, she continued. "But really, Leander, it is *too* bad of you not to give me warning. I trust you will be dining with us tonight?" she ascertained, bestowing a dazzling smile upon Arden.

"I shall be delighted," Arden returned immediately.

"And you must join us now," the dowager said. "I wish to hear what brings you here to us today."

She turned around, seeking Sir John. His eyes were on Leander and, seeing this, the dowager put her hand instead through Burnage's arm. She drew him towards the drawing room, inviting Arden to accompany them.

"You see, it is as I said," she confided to the discomfited Burnage in a tone that she must not have realised was audible to everyone. "He is such a charming man. I am sure he is maligned and is not wicked at all."

Sir John looked at Leander where they remained at the head of the stairs. "Well?"

"Do you foresee a long engagement?" Leander enquired.

Sir John's eyes were shrewd. "We will marry as soon as is possible."

"*Henry!*"

Starting forward at the dowager's shriek of alarm, Sir John checked when Leander put a hand to his arm.

"It is not serious," Leander assured him.

Sir John's lips twitched in a manner that betrayed his swift comprehension of the situation. He was solemn again almost immediately. "Your mother will have the protection of my name," he said, lowering his voice still further. "But what of you, Ockley? Do you know what you are doing here?"

Leander's expression was sober. "I believe I do, Sir John. Whatever the outcome, you must be aware that I have no desire to go abroad in society any longer."

Sir John sighed. "I cannot admit myself surprised," he confessed, following Leander into the drawing room.

The dowager was kneeling beside her younger son, who had leaned back against the sofa with a hand nursing his jaw. Arden was sprawled comfortably in a chair as he watched. Burnage perched uncertainly on the edge of another, his glance darting from Henry to Arden but not resting on either one for too long.

"How *could* you be so clumsy, Henry?" The dowager was fondly scolding him. "Leander, oblige Pickett to fetch some salve for your brother's face. He has fallen and hurt himself."

At her words, Henry looked up to see his brother standing there regarding him, and his glare was murderous. Leander conveyed the message to Pickett and took a seat in a chair beside Arden, from where he enjoyably watched the dowager fussing around Henry. It was not long before Henry firmly declared himself healed and seated her on the sofa, dismissing the salve-bearing Pickett as he did so.

"Will you be well enough to go to the Davenports' tonight?" She was anxious. "I would hate you to spoil your chances by having an ugly mark on your face, although, of course, it would take considerably more than that for you not to make the right impression. I had hoped that you might engage your interest with Annabel before returning to Spain. There is no point in looking to Louisa, as her mama agrees with me that Leander would do for her." Suddenly reminded, she turned upon Leander. "And if you do not make a push to fix your interest with her, you will find that she too has been married elsewhere while you have been dallying."

Surmising that he was still unforgiven for allowing Sophia to escape, Leander smiled amiably at his mother. "Do not worry, Mama. I shall not hold it against my brother should he wish to make a play for her."

Henry's fulminating glare filled Leander with a glow of satisfaction.

"In fact, I hope he will," Leander continued blandly, "because you should know, Mama, that you must not expect to see me wed again. If you wish for an heir, I suggest you look to Henry."

He watched with interest for a moment to see if Henry really would go off in a fit of apoplexy, then rose from his chair while his mother's mouth was still working soundlessly. Burnage's blue eyes were tragic on Henry's face, and Sir John's attention was determinedly concentrated on the clock on the mantelshelf, his lips having not yet recovered from their recently discovered tendency to twitch alarmingly.

Leander and Arden made their farewells and left.

CHAPTER TWENTY-FOUR

The drawing room at Berkeley Square was as welcoming and relaxing as Leander remembered. Once they were comfortably settled with a glass of sherry, and no servant in sight, Leander allowed the smile that had been growing inside him to blossom on his face. He could not remember such happiness as now threatened to overwhelm him—being with Arden in this way, with no misunderstandings left between them.

Save perhaps one. "I did not know you and Henry were so well acquainted."

Arden groaned. "Ever since the night Burnage invited himself to an evening of drinking and actresses, your brother has been a thorn in my flesh. He decided he could not ask for satisfaction, for to do so would cause too many questions. He set instead to making himself as annoying as possible."

And Henry, Leander knew, could be *most* annoying when he set his mind to it.

"He attempted to recruit my man. And my cook. And my head groom. Fortunately, they appear happy with such an undemanding and generous master, and they informed me of these attempts."

Leander grinned at the thought of Arden being undemanding but then realised what the man meant. He did not seem to employ the attentions of a valet very often, and cuisine was not the primary focus of the dinners he hosted.

"If I lay a bet on one prizefighter, he will always choose the opponent and crow in the most objectionable manner if his fighter wins. And then there was the occurrence at Newmarket three years ago."

"Occurrence?" Leander asked, for Arden's exasperation had sharpened into annoyance.

"Rumours were circulating that I had a ring-in for the three-year-old race. It was said that I ran an older horse, and that is why he won. I cannot be sure it was your brother's handiwork," Arden admitted. "But the accusation was absurd and your brother atrociously smug when the stewards made inquiries."

Leander was once more appalled by the depths to which Henry would sink. A foolish feud was one thing, however seriously intended, but to cast doubt on a man's honour? That went too far.

Arden laughed suddenly — self-deprecation vying with true humour. "I cannot hold myself entirely blameless," he confessed. "Although, in my defence, your brother drove me to it. There was a particular sale at Tattersall's that we both attended, and when I saw where his interest lay, I outbid him."

"Thus imposing upon yourself a horse you did not want?" Leander interpreted.

"Thus imposing upon myself *six* horses I did not want," Arden said. "Abominable screws, all of them. Towards the end of the sale, I suspected that Talbot was beginning to bid on the most appalling creatures just to bleed me. I finally allowed him to push me high and then declined to make any further bids. I believe he paid three times what that star-gazing daisy cutter was worth."

Leander laughed.

"But the Newmarket mischief," Arden mused. "For that, I do bear him ill will. He bought his commission soon after, so perhaps he knew he had gone too far, although I'm not sure what he thought my retaliation might be."

"Was I not your retaliation?" Leander asked softly.

Arden looked startled, and then his lips twisted. "I suppose you were," he said at last. "I venture that, from Talbot's perspective, my move has been successful, for I have not seen such outrage and fury in him since he heard about Burnage." He looked into his glass for a moment, surveying the golden liquid thoughtfully before his gaze raised to Leander's face once more. "I own, from my perspective, it is the most fortunate thing I have ever done."

And there was silence between them because there was no need for further words.

The dinner in Green Street had been one of the most interesting meals that Leander could remember having enjoyed around the family table. As a good host, Leander had informed Arden of his mother's preference for knee breeches at dinner. He only understood the gravity of his error when the Duke of Arden was announced, for the full glory of Arden in evening dress rendered him momentarily speechless. It was torment almost past bearing not to be able to touch him or even to stare for more than an instant at the black coat that moulded to his body as closely as did his white silk knee breeches.

The dowager had continued in her enthusiasm for Leander's new friend, although she was cool towards her eldest son following his earlier disappointing announcement. Sir John was punctiliously polite. His attitude had thawed slightly as the evening progressed and he realised that Arden was capable of behaving with propriety when he so chose. Henry and Burnage had been quiet and desirous of making an early appearance at the Davenports'.

Despite his enjoyment of the resentful silence enveloping Henry, Leander decided he must speak to his brother the following day. Now he was no longer consumed by anger and hurt, he thought he may have been too unforgiving in his suspicions and had ascribed to Henry the least worthy motives possible, when in fact he had been attempting to protect Leander. The brothers would never be close, but they did care for one another. Leander had somehow lost sight of that.

After the meal, Leander and Arden wended their way back to Berkeley Square. They retired late, drinking brandy in the drawing room long enough to give credence to the tale of Leander over-indulging and staying with a friend rather than attempting to make his drunken way home.

"So, Leander," Arden murmured, as he untied Leander's cravat. "Why shall I be spending time at Ockley? I wonder where your racehorses are stabled. Perhaps I might like to inspect them with a view to breeding with mine."

"Yes," Leander said, freeing Arden's hair from the black riband that confined it. He was not entirely sure whether he preferred Arden's hair loose and tumbling around Arden's shoulders or the feel of it trailing softly over Leander's skin, most particularly his thighs.

"Yes?" Arden asked. "That is a singularly unenlightening answer."

Leander looked up from his unbuttoning of Arden's shirt. "They are kept between Ockley and Epsom, but for the love of God, now is not the time for this discussion."

"You may not be entirely mistaken," Arden said. To Leander's great satisfaction, his voice faltered as Leander's hand glanced over the fall of his breeches. "Sit down."

Leander obediently sat on the edge of the bed. Arden knelt before him and removed his shoes. Leander's teeth sank into his lower lip as he watched Arden's bent head. Spending an entire evening with him without being able to touch had driven him almost mad. Unable to resist any longer, he wrapped his hands in Arden's hair and drew him up for a kiss, pulling him onto the bed on top of him. He rubbed against him while his hands explored desperately. Arden kissed him back, hard, then bit his lip. Leander cried out and jerked upwards, his own teeth burying in warm flesh. A sound from Arden, and Leander's hands were pinned against the bed as Arden stared down at him, breathing deeply.

"Don't be impatient, Leander," he commanded.

Leander strained upwards to rub himself against Arden's hard cock. Arden pulled back, his grip on Leander's wrists tightening. "I said no."

"God," Leander gasped in frustration. "Just fuck me, Arden."

"Oh, I will," Arden promised. He released Leander's hands so that he could draw Leander's shirt over his head before sliding back down to remove his stockings. This time Leander did not interfere. But once Arden was back on the bed, Leander's fingers went unerringly to the fall of Arden's knee breeches. Arden stopped him once more and pinned his hands above his head

"Not yet," he growled.

Leander bucked upwards beneath him, trying to dislodge him. Arden's eyes glinted as he looked at Leander. Bending his head, he kissed Leander thoroughly, so thoroughly that Leander barely noticed that Arden now held his wrists with one hand only and was feeling about on the bed with his other hand. By the time this had registered, it was too late—Arden had picked up the cravat that had been tossed onto the bed when removed from its wearer's neck and wound the length of material firmly around Leander's wrists, binding them together. He reached further and tied the ends around one of the bedposts before sliding back down Leander's body.

"Let us see you try to hurry me now," he said.

Leander's initial uncertainty at this development was assuaged by Arden's smile, and then he forgot everything except the torture of Arden's touch. Arden's lips, tongue and teeth explored every single inch of Leander's naked upper body. And then his hand glanced over the hardness in his breeches. Leander tried frantically to angle himself so that Arden would touch him there again. But all the man would do from where he was placed between Leander's open legs was trace his inner thighs through the clinging silk of his breeches. With a final desperate effort, Leander managed to move at the right moment so that Arden's hand brushed over his cock rather than his thigh. Arden instantly removed his hand, and Leander groaned in anguish.

Arden raised his head from his consideration of Leander's body to look at Leander's face. "So that's what you want, is it? Why did you not just say so?"

Leander's response would have warmed the cheeks of a hardened hackney driver. Certainly Arden seemed to think so, for he leaned forward and stopped Leander's mouth with his tongue.

As he did so, he had been unfastening the fall of Leander's breeches. Leander cried out as long fingers touched his cock, smoothing over the damp head, and then withdrew. "Please, Arden," he begged, yanking yet again at the cravat that held him mercilessly. "Please."

Arden slowly finished undoing Leander's breeches, and Leander raised his hips to allow him to pull them down. There was the briefest of pauses while Arden opened the bottle of oil, and Leander shivered in anticipation. Then he felt warm breath against his balls, followed by unspeakable delight as Arden's mouth worked them, his slicked finger slipping inside Leander

By the time Arden moved from him to finish undressing, Leander was sobbing with every breath he drew. He watched Arden's body slowly revealed in the candlelight and moaned anew, unable to tear his eyes from the dark thrusting cock.

Arden saw where he looked and knelt astride him, offering

himself to Leander. Unable to guide it with his hands, with Arden not doing so for him, the shiny head nudged clumsily against his lips where his head was raised desperately to receive it. Finally, it slid into his mouth, and he tasted Arden. He was whimpering breathlessly as he sucked, close to coming just from Arden's beautiful cock in his mouth. Arden realised, it seemed, and pulled out, leaving Leander staring imploringly up at him.

"All right, Leander." Arden's voice was soft, and then he was moving Leander up the bed slightly so that there was sufficient slack in the cravat to roll him onto his side. He pressed against him and teased a little longer before he pushed slowly inside. Leander would have moaned but for the fact he couldn't breathe. Slowly Arden began to fuck him, moving almost lazily, or so it seemed to Leander who gasped softly each time Arden slid home. One large hand curved around Leander and began to stroke his nipples while teeth grazed his shoulder and the hard cock kept sliding in and out of him, again and again.

Leander lost awareness of everything except Arden's touch and Arden's cock. He didn't even want to come any longer, just to stay like this forever. But then Arden's hand moved down, and his thumb smoothed over the wet tip of Leander's cock, causing Leander to cry out. He felt Arden's smile against his damp skin as he kissed Leander's shoulder, before the rhythm of Arden's thrusts changed, gradually becoming faster as his hand moved on Leander's cock, until Leander was sobbing his need and Arden was groaning with each thrust. "Come for me, Leander," he gasped, thrusting hard. "Come for me."

With a sobbing groan, Leander did so, his seed soaking the sheet beneath him. Moments later, Arden followed him.

They lay quietly recovering for a time before Arden kissed Leander's shoulder and pulled away. Leander turned onto his back and looked at Arden.

"I take it you intend to do something about this?" He indicated the way his hands were still fastened above his head.

Arden grinned suddenly. "Don't offer me such temptation," he threatened, before moving to work on the knots. It took him some time to work the tightly pulled material free. Leander was beginning to feel distinctly uneasy when finally Arden managed to release him. Leander brought his hands down and rubbed at stretched muscles.

Busy as he was with this, it took him a while to notice that Arden was unnaturally still on the bed beside him. He looked over at last and saw Arden staring unblinkingly at the canopy above them.

"Arden?" Leander sat up in concern. "What's wrong?"

There was a pause before Arden spoke. "Your brother may be a damned annoyance, but he was right about one thing."

"*Henry*? Right about *what*?"

Arden's lips lifted at the incredulity in Leander's voice, but he quickly sobered again.

"Your reputation. If we are seen to be close friends, you will no longer be fully welcomed by those who matter in society. So that we may be safe, I must continue my ways, presiding over orgies involving actresses and opera dancers and encouraging accounts of these to spread. That will not endear me to the *ton*—there will be no tale of a rake's redemption to soften your reception."

"I know." Leander's quiet admission brought Arden's head round to meet his gaze. "I have thought on it, believe me." How could he not have thought on the way those who professed to be his friends had been so quick to disown him? One corner of his mouth twisted as he met the painful query in Arden's eyes. "I am here, am I not? I have made my choice, although I would be obliged if you did no more at those orgies than preside."

Arden still did not relax. "Are you aware what it will mean for you?"

Leander pressed a brief kiss to his lips. "I am," he said, as he lay beside Arden once more. He had spent some time thinking about it and was at peace with the decisions he had made. "I do not wish to wed again. There will be no children, so no entrée into society will be required. Should Henry fail to produce an heir, my young cousin will inherit. He seems a sensible boy, and I will instruct him in the ways of estate management in due course. So you see, there is no need for me to give a damn about the hypocrisy of the *ton*." He hesitated, very briefly. "And every reason for me to give a damn about you. You know that I do, don't you, Arden?"

Arden's breath ceased for an instant, and then he breathed out softly, as if relinquishing a burden. "Yves," he said. "My name is Yves."

"Yves," Leander repeated, pressing a kiss onto the warm shoulder beside him.

Arden drew him close. "No one has called me that since — for many years," he said quietly.

Leander lay with his eyes closed, listening to the steady beat of Arden's heart.

"Leander." Soft breath stirred his hair.

"I know," he murmured, and Arden's arms tightened around him.

Held in the warm security of his embrace, Leander slowly drifted into a peaceful sleep.

ABOUT THE AUTHOR

Joy Lynn Fielding lives in a small English market town, where she indulges her passions for vintage aircraft, horse riding and gardening (though not all at the same time).

Joy tends to wax lyrical about the fascinating facts she discovers during her research for books. Thankfully, she has a very patient Labrador who has a gift for looking interested in what she's saying while he waits for the food to arrive.

www.ingramcontent.com/pod-product-compliance
Lightning Source LLC
Chambersburg PA
CBHW071234130626
46556CB00003B/1002